HELL ON HEELS

PRAISE FOR *HELL ON HEELS* AND LYNNE RUSSELL

"CNN's Lynne Russell is back, in an explosion of page-turning talent. Get your best bottle of wine, your favorite couch, and prepare for one wild night with *HELL ON HEELS*. It's a helluva read!"

—Craig Nelson, bestselling author of *Rocket Men* and *The First Heroes*

"P.J. Santini, the heroine of *HELL ON HEELS*, is the love child of Janet Evanovich and Elmore Leonard. Lynne Russell's spunky private eye had me at P.J.'s peeing into a one-pound coffee can during stakeouts. It is just so Jeff Bridges' burnt-out country singer in *Crazy Heart*, before the love of a good woman took all the piss out of him."

-Rita Zekas, *Toronto Star*

"Step aside Jack Reacher, PJ Santini is the new bad ass on the scene, actually a very fine ass to be precise. In *HELL ON HEELS* her debut caper she busts chops and cops, while tricked out in her push up bras, thigh highs and skimpy bikini panties...when she's not going commando. Nobody's playmate but easily a future Miss November, we can't wait for her next titillating adventure."

--Jeff Cohen, Exec Editor/ Publisher *Playboy* Special Editions, Playboy Enterprises

"*HELL ON HEELS* should come with a WARNING label! Lynne Russell's masterful depiction of female Investigator P J. Santini can literally raise your pulse rate to dangerous levels.
The brilliantly crafted insights a reader gets into the thought processes of the clever, gutsy, tough-talking, yet sexually vulnerable Santini, is alone worth the price of admission."

-Ted Kavanau, Founder of CNN HEADLINE NEWS

"Hilarious! P.J. Santini's hard-boiled detective banter is as sharp and sexy as her stilettos. A humour-mixed-with-murder mystery romp featuring a roster of brash street-smart characters, in this fast-paced riff on hard-boiled detective fiction. "

-Rhonda Rovan, Beauty Editor,
Best Health/Readers Digest Canada

"P.J. Santini is actually Lynne Russell late at night with wine, lights out, imagination gone wild. Both of them are Columbo without the cigar and appendage. Oh the joy of thinking you've been invited to ride shotgun and look for her weapons stash."

-*Moby-In-The-Morning*, Moby Enterprises

"A news anchor with the personality of a professional wrestler."

-*The New York Times*

"Talk about a Renaissance woman, Lynne Russell does it all!"

-Warner Bros. Television

The 1st P.J. Santini Series Book

LYNNE RUSSELL

ABOUT THE AUTHOR

LYNNE RUSSELL ANCHORED *CNN* and *CNN Headline News* from 1983 to 2001, the first woman to solo anchor a network nightly newscast. Her long-standing dedication to the people's right to know was recognized in *The New York Times,* which called her a "just-the-facts stalwart of CNN Headline News". The *Times* also called her a news anchor with the personality of a professional wrestler, which she took as a compliment. In the *Washington Journalism Review*, she won a spot as "Best in the Business". A private investigator and former deputy sheriff, Lynne now writes romantic crime novels. She and her husband split their time between Washington, D.C. and Italy.

PJ Santini lives in an uncharted corner of Lynne's brain. When PJ spends long, boring hours stuck in a car on a surveillance job, she amuses herself by counting all the places on her body where she can stash her gun – she's up to twelve now – and she wishes to thank Lynne for the idea. It helps to make up for the indignity of having to pee into a one-pound coffee can.

ABOUT HELL ON HEELS

QUIRKY AND WITTY, HELL ON HEELS is fast-moving recommended reading for those who crave danger and passion in life, but still want to be home by dinner.

Welcome to blistering summertime in Buffalo, New York, scene of the crime. Thirty-three year old PJ Santini, television news reporter and marginally successful private eye, is on a wild ride between men, her certifiable Sicilian family and insufficient funds notices, ever since her husband died on her – literally. But good news, she's inherited the juicy journalistic job of Gerald Sigmund (Siggy), a sleezy investigative reporter who has vanished into thin air. Her first assignment is to find him, dead or alive. She's also inherited his disgusting office, which holds a secret that's worth her life. But she has no idea what that secret is, or who would kill her to get to it. All she knows is that there's a bloody finger in the desk drawer, and it lost most of its value as evidence when she threw up all over it.

Her only comforts are Chianti, four-inch heels and chocolate. And two men. Fiercely protective Tango Daly is her mysterious, tanned, toned private detective boss, a martial artist with a para-legitimate past tucked lustily into seductive slacks and silk shirts. They play exhilarating mind games when her stilettos get caught in the thick carpet of his office. Upstairs, the place is equipped with more surveillance electronics than Cheyenne Mountain...and a bed with satin sheets.

Lanky Johnny Renza is darkly handsome in his trademark cream linen suit, and the first boy PJ ever loved... over and over, all through high school. Now he's a top-notch, competitive crime reporter who gets away with plenty because he still knows how to hotwire her with fattening food. As her butt is about to get its own zip code, it's getting harder to concentrate on staying alive.

DEDICATION

For Concetta

ACKNOWLEDGEMENTS

MANY THANKS TO MY GOOD friend and mentor in the business of private investigation and security, Keith Flannigan, for his invaluable insight, technical advice, patience and sense of humor; and to the people of Buffalo, New York for sharing their city, their unstoppable attitude, and their Italian heritage and food!

ONE

"DIDN'T YOU FORGET SOMETHING?" This private detective boss misses nothing. "They *will* ticket you, if you don't feed the meter."

"No problem," I said. "As of a few minutes ago, I'm also a member of the media. Don't you see the big PRESS sign on the dashboard?"

"Don't you see the blue-and-white up the street?"

"Five bucks says he passes."

"You don't have five bucks."

"Do so." I slapped four ones on his desk, and the three quarters, two dimes and a nickel that would have been parking money.

"I hate to do this Janice, I really do, but you've got to learn," he said as he lifted his toned, tan body out of the chair and pulled a wallet loaded with fifties from his back pants pocket. "Can you make change?" He caught my wrist just as I reached for the big Swarovski crystal paperweight. He'd stepped up his workouts, you could tell right through the silk.

"Your name sure isn't Patience, is it Janice?"

"It isn't Janice, either," as I went for the letter opener. He vice-gripped *that* wrist, and it felt like a million bucks.

"Now what are you going to do?" His eyes were bright with confidence. I was gulping air, inhaling his vitality, taking in the expensive, soft black short-sleeve shirt just slightly darker than his close-cropped hair. He had sea-green eyes and a twelve-month healthy glow.

My gaze just naturally traveled down his pants, because any smart woman would want to maximize the dollars she'd put into her self-defense training; but we were on opposite sides of the desk. "I know," he said leaning over to croon in my ear, "but you wouldn't really do it. You like it like this. I make you hot."

It was a terrible curse. My breathing was labored from the proximity to him and everything he represented – control, excitement, experience, knowledge, mystery, drop-dead sexiness. To save myself, I exercised my only option: I sank my teeth into his ear.

"Ow! Damn, girl, if you missed a meal just say so!" With his hand clamped up to the side of his head, I couldn't tell whether I'd drawn blood or not. Suddenly he looked like a little boy and I wished I had defended my honor without hurting him. I went around to check.

"You all right? I didn't mean to..."

He took a fast step toward me – the martial artist in him ever alert – and we were nose to nose, breathing the same air again. His high heel-eating plushy carpet wouldn't turn me loose, and I didn't care. This was not the first time we'd played this game, yet I never got any better at it. I wasn't convinced I really wanted to, and still hadn't worked out whether or not he would eventually let me win. All I knew was that he was Tango Daly, the heart and soul of my new adopted home, Iroquois Investigations; the man bad guys hated, women loved and I absolutely... I didn't let myself think about that.

I'm PJ Santini, also known as Janice because my real name is too embarrassing. I'm pretty sure I'm the private eye with the most pairs of four-inch heels in the Tri State Area. I'm also a frequently out-of-work television journalist, mother of a car and a condo I can't afford, daughter of a wacked-out Sicilian earth mother and a retired police sergeant who isn't really retired, and a widow after only two days of marriage. That's right, two days.

"Marry him," Ma had said. "Men are like linoleum. Lay him right the first time... if you can even remember the first time..."

"Ma!"

"...and you can walk all over him the rest of your life." Or for two days.

More importantly, I admit to being slave to the overall lure of dangerous men and dark chocolate. Also I'm probably schizophrenic, since this is beginning to make perfect sense. Unfortunately all that sense isn't sitting inside a killer body. At 5'9", I'm too tall to be short and too short to be tall. I'd say my distinguishing feature is the completely off-the-hook curly red hair that rests on my shoulders, except in summer when it frizzes up a good two inches. You can see why I'm grateful for any positive attention.

So far, it had been a day of abnormally positive attention, and this was beginning to scare me. It all began right after I got up when, in desperate need of more income, I'd swallowed my pride, along with three cups of coffee, double-double, and a hefty shot of Jack Daniels. I put on matching underwear and ran a blouse through the touch-up cycle in the dryer. Ten ambitious hair rollers burned off dust as they fired up in the bathroom. I moussed and sprayed my hair into submission, and an hour later was in office of the news director at the television station I'd worked at three years earlier. Murray Soper was his name, and I was primed to grovel for a spot on his chain gang. Little did I know that his infamous investigative reporter Gerald Sigmund had mysteriously disappeared, and Soper was one inmate short. All I had to do was ask.

"I just gave the dipshit a month's advance, and now he's gone," Soper whined, eyeing me through the little finger teepee executives make when they want to look brilliant. He was doing what they all do, sizing up the peon trapped in his office, calculating how little he could get me for. I felt more insignificant by the second, sinking deeper into the ratty sofa opposite his big shiny desk. His office was set up like this on purpose, because he had a thing about being short. Not just Boy's Department short, but booster seat short. His mom had squeezed out a store sample, and Murray never stopped taking it personally. The couch was his revenge. So was the desk, which was propped up on four inches of beer coasters. The chair behind it was jacked up so high his toes barely tickled the shag.

The spasm I was getting in my neck from looking up at him was intimidating, but I decided I'd make up for it later. Right now I really needed money, and the truth was he could get me for a lot less than he thought. I watched in the long silence, as his teeth worked through the dry skin on his lip. When they drew blood, I had to say something.

"Any idea where he went?" I asked, reaching around to tug at my thong. I get nervous around people who can't handle stress. I have found that where there's stress there's shooting, and a lot of the time it's at me.

"I'm clueless," he said, and I totally believed him. "*Find him, damn it Santini, find him*!"

Alright, already. Watching this performance I was mystified, as usual, over what makes males tick. All my life, I've been too willing to give them what they wanted. Take Johnny Renza. It's my personal opinion he's the reason I sucked my thumb into fourth grade. Our families were close from day one, meaning our mothers changed our diapers side-by-side, over and over. This was a recipe for disaster. At such an impressionable age, a girl looks often enough at a hunk like him under those circumstances, and something's gonna get sucked.

By my fourth birthday party, his wish was my command. When Renza wanted to go into the broom closet and play Touch Where the Light Shines, I went and got a flashlight. When I turned twelve I was still under his spell, although I had the thumb sucking under control. We played the broom closet again, but somehow the meaning was different. Plus, he had more hands than I'd remembered. This was when I realized that whatever you think a man wants, he's really after. more.

"Are you listening? I want you to replace Siggy, that idiot, as investigative reporter. Immediately and permanently!" I slapped myself back into the present. Soper was so worked up he was frothing. "Your first assignment is to find him. *Find Gerald Sigmund*." His palm slapped the desk in rhythm with Ger-ald Sig-mund.

"Tsh. You must be joking. You hire *me* to find another reporter? That's impossible! What am I, psychic? Where would I look for a guy like Siggy?" Then I added, to sound knowingly nonchalant, "He don't run with the traffic." I was sure this would stop him in his tracks. It didn't.

"You're the private eye, break it down," he insisted. "Job's going fast, take it or leave it." This was not working out as I had planned. I just wanted a job... not, you know, *A JOB*. I picked at my nails. It'd be nice to afford a manicure again. And I could, by sandwiching a few TV news reports in between Daly's investigative skip traces, and picking up a regular paycheck.

He took aim at the floor and jumped from his chair, stomping imaginary bugs. "What kind of investigative reporter leaves you high and dry?" Rumpelstiltskin wanted to know. "This isn't the first time he's been a horse's arse. Santini, you can produce your own reports on this, at your own pace. Just be available so we can use you for breaking news, too. Siggy's paycheck will be yours. Clear?"

I blinked. Arse? I was going to work for a man who said *arse?* "Fine." I didn't even ask about the money, it didn't matter. I'd take whatever crumbs he'd throw my way. He couldn't throw many, this being the thirteenth-rated station in the twelve-station Buffalo, New York market. He lobbed Siggy's keys at me, told me which office it was, and I was outta there before he could say that word again. I'll do a lot for a paycheck, but I have a low tolerance for arse.

Heading down the hall I ticked off my priorities, what I like to call PJ's Three P's: payday, personal calls and privacy. And I did a mental rewind of the three years since I'd left the station. Back then, Lester Shula – otherwise known as Poppin' Fresh – had been in charge of the newsroom. He got the name inhaling something that looked a lot like flour in the break room. Shula had presided over a news operation with more backstabbing than junior cheerleader tryouts.

Just one thing could make it worse: his daughter. Kathy Shula was the high-maintenance little bitch who made me miserable all through school. Look up *perky* in any dictionary, and there's her picture. Then we both went to the University at Buffalo, where she of course stole my major, Journalism. She got straight A's, while I was struggling along in the C-section.

Then we both wound up working for her father. Or rather, I should say I worked... I wrote, I edited, I shot video, I reported. She perfected her eyeliner and her thousand-yard stare at the TelePrompter. It drove me nuts. It also drove me to church. I thought if I racked up enough novenas, CBS would snatch me up and elevate me to a glamorous life in the fast lane of the Big Apple. High profile exclusive stories, personal hairdresser, limo to work, six-figure starting salary. My sweet face plastered on billboards across America.

But it didn't happen. Lou Bonmarito happened. Lou was a blind date that caught fire and melted my underwear. Ten seconds later, I quit the newsroom, set up five bridal registries and got married. I was pretty sure I loved him. He had a great future at his law firm, and he knew a stock from a bond, and a wood from an iron. I'm told this is important to adults. Plus, he was cuter than a basket of puppies, and he appreciated the valuable assets hunkered just beneath my ordinary surface.

There really isn't much more to say about Lou, except that I was trying to be practical for once in my life. I admit my first love was Renza, and that has never changed. But my biological clock was ticking like a time bomb, and Renza wasn't the marrying kind. I needed a guy who could see past next week, a guy who was dependable but sort of elegant, like a late model Mercedes S-class. Renza was more of a prom night stretch limo with a sparkly paint job, stocked bar with crystal glasses, three TV's, six doors and two moon roofs... alluring, lusty and built for the present... with eight ways out, but you don't want to take any of them even though you know you should.

When Pop walked me down the aisle and we passed Renza, I fumbled the bouquet trying to stick my thumb in my mouth under the veil. Obviously that was a bad omen, because on the second day of our honeymoon on Maui, Lou went and died on me. Literally, on me. It was humiliating. At my parents' house after the funeral, Kathy Shula siphoned up a beaker of red wine at the food table.

"We all know he only married her to look solid at the firm," Kathy said. "Their sex was nothin' extra... he told me!" Everybody stopped chewing. "Turns out, she bored him right into a coma. He'd still be alive – really alive, if you get my drift – if he were married to me." She really knew how to work a crowd. The women emptied their glasses. The men watched, fascinated, as she tongued deviled egg off the roof of her mouth. "Ya know in Italian, Bonmarito means good husband. Louie obviously couldn't face living up to *that* one." Some of the men nodded yes. After that, I wanted to leave town. I just never got packed.

When Lou's microscopic life insurance payout was exhausted, I'd rather have cut the White House lawn with nail scissors than beg Kathy's father to give me my old job back. So I had an unusually meaningful and productive conversation with myself.

"You like to eat, right? And drink?" I asked.

"Um, right."

"And you're no stranger to the shoe department of every major store, designer boutique and factory outlet, true?"

"Uh sure, so what's your point?"

"These things cost money. You don't have any. Think of a way to get some."

"You mean... *work?*" I freaked myself out, and had to open a bottle of red for medicinal purposes.

"Exactly. And don't even think of trying to sell your body. That ship has left the dock. Your ass gets any bigger, somebody's going to slap a Wide Load triangle on it."

"Very funny," I told the bitch.

"However, you do have some assets. You're naturally inquisitive... nosy, in fact... and sneaky. These things make you a good reporter. They could also make you a good private investigator." And the rest is industry history. I became a private eye, and it almost paid the bills.

Time rolled on, and it rolled right over the TV station. Ratings went into the dumper. After a lengthy and embarrassing trial, Poppin' Fresh was sent to the Big House for selling cocaine to the janitorial crew in the parking lot. Out of respect, I waited a decent period of time – about half a day – and contacted his replacement, Murray Soper, for another crack at reporting.

After our meeting, I scuttled out of his office with the keys, to find the room that had been Siggy's. Luckily, Siggy had abandoned an unattractive, windowless hole that nobody in their right mind would want. Except me, and here's why: It was so far away from the Suits, it was almost in the parking lot. It was also conveniently located just down the hall from my other office, the restroom. I pushed that door open first, and noticed the old sign was still there. *Women*. Before that, it had said *Ladies*; but Poppin' Fresh gathered us all together one day to tell us he thought *Ladies* was demeaning.

"Plus," he said with a sly smile, "everybody knows there are no ladies in *this* newsroom." So many people eyeballed his daughter, he ended the meeting.

"Anybody home?" I echoed as I took in the new institutional yellow paint job and brown tile floor. It made me want to order tacos.

"Can't be. Is that you, Janice? I heard you were coming in!" The voice interrupted piddling to wait for an answer, and I knew who it was. Cherry Snyder had the best bladder control in the building. She could knock down five cups of coffee, then hit the bathroom and carry on a complete conversation between punctuating blasts. She also used to date Gerald Sigmund.

"Yep, back at the scene of the crime," I said watering down my hands and smoothing my hair. "Picking up where Siggy left off, wherever that was." Siggy was known as an eccentric but gutsy reporter. That normally excuses most people's twisted behavior, and some of his. He also had a reputation as a womanizer, a man who went after what he wanted with the tenacity of a hive of Georgia yellow jackets that's been whacked five times with a baseball bat. For awhile, what he wanted was Cherry.

"Well before you ask," she said, "I don't know where he is, *and I still don't care.*"

"Still the same reason?" I asked.

"Still the same. My gynecologist's writing it up for a medical journal."

I could sympathize. On one occasion I'd shared *one* drink with him for *one* hour, which was about fifty-nine minutes longer than it took to be absolutely positive we had no future together. Afterward, the rash on my collarbone where he kissed me goodnight didn't clear up for five days.

When I left Cherry, she was giving a whole new meaning to pissed off. I unlocked my new office door and hit the lights – which had been left on, so as a courtesy to me they immediately went off. While they were sputtering back, I off-loaded an armful of manila folders crammed with story ideas onto the visitor's chair, and topped it off with my impressive camel-colored fake alligator attaché. The chair groaned, debated, then spewed the whole thing into the grimy darkness under Siggy's desk. This was a place I did not want to go.

I'm not sure why I held my nose, it just seemed like the right thing to do. As I fished around for the files, it occurred to me that many a news star has been born kneeling in a strange office in the dark. But then, nobody was watching them. I, on the other hand, was crawling around with my good straight skirt riding up around my ribcage with the door open. When the fluorescents finally powered up, the whole newsroom got an eyeful of my butt. I imagined it took up the entire doorway. Oh my god, did control top pantyhose have a see-through crotch? Had I put on underwear? I couldn't remember. They were looking at something I'd never seen myself, and I wondered if the smirking meant it was good or bad.

Recovering from this was going to take attitude. Fortunately, Buffalo women are born with a lifetime supply. Visitors coochie-coo newborns in the hospital nursery, and girl babies come back with *You got somethin' you wanna say to me?* So I straightened up and smoothed down the fabric like I didn't care, and wiped the sweat from my upper lip. "Next time, I'm charging admission, assholes!" When the crowd disbursed, I contemplated taking a work break. My watch said it was only 9:23 AM. I bet if I slammed it hard enough into a wall it'd say something else.

I limped around the desk past the sign that warned "Gerald Sigmund, Investigative Reporter. Be afraid." and plopped into his big cement-colored leather chair. At one time it could have been a burnished brown, the stains made it hard to tell. It glided over to the computer, which like the lights, had been left on.

I could tell the desk was Siggy's by the things I was peeling off and launching into the trash. Stickie notes with girls' names and meaningful notations: Rack, Legs, Cream. I took a wild guess these were not graduates of the Buffalo School of Fine Cuisine. When I got to Pearl Necklace and Golden S, I took another guess they weren't jewelers, either. No-Tell-Motel numbers were scratched on a piece of faded cardboard stuck under the phone. I had to pry it off with a pen.

All of this was curious, because ordinarily companies too inefficient to spell your name right in Payroll, are Johnny-on-the-spot when it comes to clearing out your entire office when you're history. This would include jacking your hard drive before it gets cold. But it looked like everything of Siggy's was still here. His Rolodex was sitting behind the phone. Next to it was a more or less round, pock-marked brown container of paper clips that looked like a hollowed out turd.

"Yo, Deadeye, some grip you got on that weapon. And welcome back to ground zero." OMG, it was Johnny Renza. All grown up into an excellent reporter, but most of all, a heartache waiting to happen. To prevent this, I slapped myself hard to keep from fantasizing.

"I wish you'd stop calling me that. And don't creep around the corner. It's... creepy. How'd you find out, anyway?"

"Everybody knows. There was an office pool about which body part you'd shoot off."

"Very funny." He was making reference to my recent amazing good fortune at the firing range. I'd gotten a stick-on nail caught in the trigger and dropped the gun – again. Contrary to popular belief, it did not discharge, and nobody bled out.

The gun is a private detective perk. The license comes with a cozy little concealed weapons permit. It lets you carry, in case some genius you're staking out wants to use his sawed off shotgun to separate you from your vital signs. My personal favorite is a convenient .385 Sig-Sauer. Smooth, easy to conceal on a woman's body. When I'm working surveillance and get bored, I think of all the places it can go. I'm up to twelve. Then I run through the Great Lakes, the Hawaiian

Islands and Snow White's dwarfs, slipping in Sleazy, Gimpy and Moe just to mix things up.

Renza inched further into my cave. "Find anything freaky? I got Animal Control and HAZMAT on one touch dial," he said.

"What the hell, did he get *dragged* out of here? All his stuff's all over the place."

"Happened two days ago. The ones who know aren't saying."

"Only two days? Smells longer. No wonder the lights didn't want to come back. So where is he?"

"Who knows. AWOL, AA, NA, FTA, DOA, Costa Rica."

"Why Costa Rica?" I asked. The first five sounded too logical for Siggy.

"Only a thought. Forget it." Can't help it, along with being crazy about Renza, I actually like him. He knows when to shut up. But he says a lot, even when he isn't talking. In this kind of summer weather, he's partial to a trademark cream linen suit with matching pocket hankie. And a Mediterranean complexion like his can get a surf's-up tan just pirouetting in the parking lot. At City Hall, gaggles of cub reporters named Tiffany and Hillary get collective flashes so hot their nail polish peels. To date, in my renewed single state, the anti-Renza hermetic seal around my body was holding; but oh, I missed him from the years before I met my husband, and that made him dangerous.

"What was Siggy working on?" I asked, wriggling around in the chair like they do in the movies, to coax the cracked leather into molding to my own shape.

"Dunno. Big, big freakin' mystery, as always." He was irritated Siggy might have snagged a story dangerous enough to get him fired or dead. Renza also gets his jollies probing where he doesn't belong. Their rivalry is legendary.

"Jealous?" I asked.

"Right now a lot, but only of his chair."

"When did you start saying freakin'?" I said, cheerfully shoving Siggy's dump truck load of papers over the side. Five minutes ago, they mattered. "Getting soft, giving up real words for play ones?"

"I don't know you well enough to say fuck."

"You said it last night."

"Yeah, but you weren't listening."

My intuition was, and it told me he had not gotten soft, or changed at all, since those fast times at St. Agatha of Catania – where boys were boys, and girls were locked up. Except in Vicky Balducci's rec room. Vicky was my best friend and still is, a straight-haired, blonde version of moi. If we could clone ourselves one brunette, we'd be the Witches of East Side. Her parties were like anatomy field trips. There was even the occasional final exam.

So here's the problem: I'm not a cute little thing anymore. The Italian bum is kicking in, and Ma loves to torture me with it. "A minute in the mouth, a lifetime on the hips," she says as she force-feeds me Fettuccini Alfredo. Renza can make me feel like a supermodel, but after all this time could he still mean it? Last night, dinner with him was all I could afford.

I turned back to the grey metal desk. The top right drawer wouldn't budge. It wasn't locked, it was stuck. It looked like something drippy had sealed it. My trusty Swiss army knife, one of a girl's best friends, almost had it open – but the fumes made my eyes water. "Want some help?" Renza offered. The last thing I needed was him poking around in my drawers.

Let me rephrase that. I was an investigative reporter, as much in direct competition with him as Siggy had been. What was in this desk was mine, now. I just hoped it was non-addictive, and alive only if it was supposed to be. I didn't want to share it. Anyway, I wasn't going in without a priest, or Mr. Clean. Since I was fresh out of priests, I made a mental note to stop at the store for the strongest legal disinfectant I could find.

"Okay, enough for today. Beat it, will you? I've got work to do and you're making me forget what it is."

He smiled and made his hand into a gun, "Later, Deadeye," and blew on his finger. A little voice in my head screamed *Wait, I know how to do that!*

I held my breath until he was gone, then reached down and dug the Stickies and cardboard motel list back out of the trash, and stuffed them into the middle drawer. Maybe throwing them away wasn't such a good idea. It was almost as if the office were a living, breathing thing, and it had something to say. I grabbed my attaché, and out of habit hit the light switch.

"Damn!" I shouted into the new darkness, and locked up behind me. More so nothing could get out, than the other way around.

It was pretty cool having a media parking pass in my hot little hand again. "Hi, Sweet Boy," I crooned to the car, inhaling deeply of downtown Buffalo's rich exhaust. I eased onto the soft beige leather seat of my Mercedes SLK sports car, and didn't mind at all that the heat made my skin smoke. It was a smart little silver hardtop convertible, totally inappropriate for snowy Buffalo winters, not to mention low-key investigative work. Although I'd inherited it from the husband I never got a chance to break in, I'd had better luck with the car and was driving it a lot. But it was racking up astronomical maintenance and gasoline bills.

"Look what we have, our very own parking space. Also, if we're very careful how we use it, this nifty PRESS sign for on-street parking. Let's go test it at the office."

That was when I'd headed over to see Tango Daly for some cardio mind-fucking, and to deliver the results of five days of shadowing a really horny wayward husband. Iroquois Investigations is where I hang whatever hat I'm wearing that day... skip tracer, debugger, bodyguard with a black belt, unfaithful husband bait, stuff you don't dress up for. Except that last one, unfaithful husband bait, in which case less clothing is more. Daly hadn't seen me in a business suit in a month of Sundays. I hope it wouldn't torpedo my kick-ass image. I eased Sweet Boy out of employee parking and wound around to The Strip, otherwise known as Elmwood Avenue. Iroquois occupies all of a small, nondescript two-story building in the middle of a block of small, nondescript two-story buildings. This is on purpose. Difficult to notice, easy to forget.

We pulled up to the usual meter, right in front. I whipped out the big shiny sign, and slapped it on the dashboard. Nice three-inch Day-Glo orange letters on white. A sign like that could be a cop magnet, except that this one was designed to keep the cops away. And I felt lucky.

Daly sat behind his desk at the far end of the room. This was what I imagined God's office would look like. Burgundy carpeting so thick my heels got stuck in it, matching damask drapes and lavishly framed landscapes against cream-colored walls. Behind his desk were banks of citations from past lives he didn't talk about, one or two of them very military, flanked by a couple more with a little something missing in the way of identifiable letterhead.

This was only the part of Daly's private domain that showed. The others were off-limits, especially the second floor. Iroquois Investigations had a total of fifteen door locks and three gun safes, and beside him nobody was allowed in, except his operatives. He kept everybody else at arm's length, meeting them in their own offices or in diners all over Buffalo. His reasoning was that he was dealing with the most off-center carbon-based life forms on the planet. And those were just the clients.

About the time my heels got caught in the carpet that day, something caught Daly's eye. He nodded toward the front window. Sure enough, a cop was writing Sweet Boy a ticket.

"Like I said," Daly grinned, "your are on their list. Ever since the Chaminsky case."

I watched through the open doorway, out of breath, with Daly's red fingerprints on my wrist and my shoes in my hand. "Hey PJ, how's it goin'?" the cop smirked, looking past me to see if Daly had all his clothes on.

"Why are you doing this, Wolenski? I'm here on official media business." I was challenging one of Buffalo's finest, a policeman I'd run into before. A year ago, I'd been tracking a guy making off with a client's company secrets, and I met Wolenski accidentally when I rear-ended his squad car. "Does it have anything do to with that teeny little problem in low visibility on Ashfield, officer?" Playing dumb was coming easier and easier.

"It was Ashland. And my lights were on. The sun was shining."

And the ticket was on my car under the windshield wiper, covering up my as yet virgin PRESS pass. I had to do something to save face, so I threw him, "You're just jealous because I have a gun, too." What did I have to lose?

"I'm still working on that one, sweetie." Wolenski hit his siren, gave it a little whup-whup, and took off. I was going to hate the smug look on Daly's face.

Sure enough he looked like the cat that ate the canary, so I changed the subject and said it fast. "Got the press pass at the old station. I showed up for a meeting this morning, and guess what, they hired me! Gerald Sigmund hasn't been in for two whole days, nobody knows where he is, and they don't like having an absentee reporter. So I've got a steady paycheck coming in. I suppose this means that now I'll have to pretend to work in *two* places."

"I know."

"How could you? I just came from there." Watching him lean back against the desk, his legs crossed at the ankle, his hands indifferently resting in his pants pockets, it was all I could do to remember what we were talking about. My compass was spinning. Twice in one morning, two different men, what the hell?

"It's a small world," he said, "and Sigmund is not exactly a Boy Scout. BPD is officially sitting on it, but it looks like both Vice and Homicide are very interested in talking to him. You interested too?"

"Are you kidding? If he showed up again, he could get them to give him his job back, and I need it. I just want to know which dumpster he's living in."

"Beautiful *and* mercenary. I like that in a woman."

I tried a disarming smile. "So what are you really thinking, Daly?"

"His girlfriend didn't know he was going anywhere. Says he left a note that didn't make sense."

"Who says she says? Have you talked to her?"

"*People* say. Meanwhile, you have my reports ready? It's going to go to court," he said.

I pulled a folder out of my attaché and handed it to him. It was a really snappy write-up of surveillance details for a divorce case. Everything I saw the husband do, minute by minute, every day I'd observed him. And I included as much information as I could dig up about everyone he talked to. I knew his routine like I'd know my own, if I actually had one. I'd also done a financial search, and run a background check for any past or present illegal activity – local, state, federal. Those internet background sites are cute, but they don't scratch the surface when it comes to the real interesting stuff. You need a professional.

With this case, there had been a strong possibility of reconciliation and I thought all the work was going to be for nothing. Then the missus saw the artful photos I brought back of her husband living like he was single... in the bed of a '99 Ford F-150 pick-up, with a nineteen-year-old fish fry waitress. Daly leafed through the material, slowing at pictures of the couple. He stopped at the long lens close-up of the man's hand reaching through her white uniform blouse to hold her milky breast up to his mouth, as his tongue lingered on the tip of her nipple. He stared at it.

"What, too much detail? Not enough?" I asked him. It was a great shot, if I say so myself. It even captured the moisture on his tongue.

Daly's attention crept off the paper, and he took forever contemplating the front of my suit jacket... mentally undoing one button after the other. By the time he got to the bottom, I'd broken out in a sweat and my head felt all fizzy. "Isn't today your birthday?" he asked.

I swallowed. His gaze was cool and steady. I didn't want to blink and miss anything. I was a breath away from asking for my present, when... damn... the outer pocket of my briefcase vibrated with the muffled sounds of the theme from The Godfather. It was my new text message alert. I had mixed emotions about looking, and only peeked because it might be the newsroom.

But it was Ma again, the third time since 7:30 am. The first was to wish me Happy Birthday, which was unnecessary since we'd just talked for thirty incoherent minutes, and anyway I wanted to forget everything about it. The second told me I shouldn't feel bad about getting older, as some nice man would come along. She didn't say nice *young* man anymore, just man. And she wanted to remind me we're eating at 4:30. Nobody eats dinner at 4:30 in the afternoon... except the Santinis, who have been doing it since the Dead Sea was only sick.

"Hit me hard with a frying pan, next time I give my mother a new way to track me down," I told him over my shoulder. I was trying to sound cool, but my post-nipple-picture heart rate was through the roof.

"Would this be the same technologically advanced mother who drove the car in second gear for ten years, because she thought D was for Don't?"

"Yes, it would. She didn't need a cell in the first place. She can't even program the VCR. This texting... she's like a sixth grader."

We both knew the small talk meant nothing, that the spell hadn't been broken, and we'd be back there again. The only question was whether I'd want to replay the whole crystal paperweight scenario, or pick up where we left off.

I chucked the phone into the outside of the attaché, while he stuffed something into the pocket next to it. Hopefully some of those fifties. Since I needed it, I pretended not to see.

"One fine, kick-ass woman," Daly whistled softly as he unlocked the heavy door to the upstairs and secured the outside entry behind me. I didn't even want to know what was going on up on the second floor. I'd been there only once, for just a few minutes. The room had more electronic equipment and soundproofing than Cheyenne Mountain. It also had a refrigerator and a double bed with buttery silk sheets. Enough said.

On the street, Sweet Boy was still smarting from being hit with a parking ticket. I hoped he didn't blame me. In my mind it still wasn't my fault, the damn Chaminsky case would always take the rap. Some cops just can't take being upstaged by a P.I. This car was my only extravagance...next to every girl's favorite economy size bag of Hershey kisses with almonds. To me, self control isn't laying off candy. It's holding off on chewing until you suck all the way down to the crunchy nut. And then washing it down with only one sip of champagne. At a time.

With hours to go before the command birthday appearance at Ma and Pop's, I debated being a responsible employee and going back to the television station that had just hired me – but the urge passed. Then I thought about going home; but being alone on my birthday would be depressing. Plus, home is where I stash my best high calorie surveillance provisions, including original flavor potato chips, Goldfish crackers, gummy bears and Twinkies. It's important to nourish yourself as you camp for long hours in parking lots, listening to books on tape and taking pictures of cheating spouses. It makes up for the indignity of having to pee into a one-pound coffee can.

Or, I could show uncharacteristic discipline and jog on the treadmill in front of the television, without watching the Food Network. But when you're dressed up and look this hot, you ought to be someplace where people can appreciate you. A shopping mall, for instance. Or a shoe warehouse.

I aimed the car eastward toward the Cheektowaga mall. My stocking feet began twitching at the thought of clandestine encounters with fascinating, forbidden pumps and thin-heeled sandals that could try their luck in Daly's office.

TWO

FOUR HOURS, ONE CHEESECAKE Factory mud pie and three pairs of heels from the 70% off rack later, I tossed everything into the trunk of the SLK. The shoes, especially the red ones, looked fabulous in a hooker sort of way, next to my private detective gear... jeans, hard hat, clipboard, wigs to cover my wacko hair, plain glasses and colored contact lenses.

The convertible hard top was up in the 260-degree July heat, and the AC blasted ice pellets as I headed over to face the family. Don't get me wrong, I love my relatives and fully realize my family is no more screwed up than anybody else's. In fact so many families are dysfunctional, it'd take less time to identify the ones that aren't. But Ma and Pop's grown kids have never flown very far from the nest. My brother Tony moves back in every time a relationship ends. In Ma's eyes her baby boy can do no wrong, so she cooks, cleans and picks up in a way no rational girlfriend ever would. Then there's undomesticated me, thirty-three years old and not even pregnant with a Santini grandchild. I can remember when that was a good thing.

I started thinking about Siggy's disappearance. His twisted little smirk kept popping into my head. A character like him doesn't just drop off the face of the earth, *he tells* somebody he's dropping. If he had to go undercover and not be seen on the air, or even anywhere near the station, Soper would know about it. Renza's words came back: "The ones who know aren't saying."

I took Broadway as far as Greene and swung into Lovejoy, hanging a left on Casanova. Lovejoy is a five-by-ten-block slice of Buffalo hunkered in a nest of train tracks that calls itself Iron Island. I've always thought of it as a she. *Her* wrought iron porch rails and chain link fences are not new, but she takes good care of herself and is just very experienced. The people are solid, patriotic, working class and proud of it. Lawns have a buzz cut, American flags are out, and now and again a yellow ribbon goes up around a tree. You can hang out in front of the pizzeria on a summer afternoon with a gelato. Or sit on the curb by the indoor pool, and wait for the fire truck to come barreling out of the red brick Engine 28 station across the road. Also in Lovejoy, beer is dear. There's even a street called Longnecker.

Every time I look at the narrow brown clapboard house where I grew up, it gets smaller. And darker. Dawn never comes here. In the cold months, the sky takes it personally if any light slips through the aluminum gloom. The rest of the year, full-grown maple trees drop what's left of the sun-starved front lawn into deep shadow. Still, it's been able to manufacture a tiny patch of green.

It warmed my heart to see the bald back of Pop's head through the dining room window... motionless, focused, waiting for food to drop onto the plate in front of him. In the stubby shrubs below the window, the plaster statue of St. Francis and his birds had been there for as long as I could remember. My brother's familiar footsteps came around the corner.

"What're you doin' in the bushes?" Tony asked.

"Just thinking about that Christmas the angels went bye-bye."

"Uh ho, that was really somethin', eh? What kinda guy boosts a coupla angels? That was our whole Nativity scene." It was the year Tony was fourteen and I was sixteen. St. Francis was surrounded by glorious cement angels that Ma had decided to paint Halo Gold. But there was a little accident, and in the end Tony was the hero of the day.

"Be honest Jan, you can say it now. Do you have an awesome, cool brother or what? Did it all by myself." I hugged him and had to admit he'd pulled off the big one.

His arch enemy to this day, Frank Longoria, had swiped Ma's angels on Christmas Eve morning, and left puke-green plastic toads in their place. For this travesty, there would be retribution. That evening, comes the big annual Christmas Eve tour of the Island, and everybody's shrieking when they get to the Longoria house. Frank's mom's prize-winning animated project has been rearranged, compliments of my brother. Her entire reindeer team is cluster-humping in a glorious blaze of multicolored twinkling lights. Rudolph's shiny red nose is rhythmically goosing a fat, laughing Santa who's bent over a present. Every goose almost knocks him off his chubby, pointy-toed feet. You can almost hear him squeal.

"Yeah," I said, "but next morning there was payback at *our* house. Up till then, the lawn looked normal." Our nice, snowy yard had been spray painted an Italian word for "Up yours, goombah", which could be another reason the grass has retreated.

As it happened, Nonna – which means grandma – was visiting from Sicily. Nonna Giovanna is my father's mother, and one tough cookie. In her case, Nonna means here comes trouble. Before anybody could stop her, she was out in the snow in her black shawl, black dress, black wool stockings and black combat boots setting fire to a pile of wood the size of a Buick to "erase the curse". To this day, when you sit on the grass in hot weather you can smell gasoline. In Lovejoy, even the greenery has to be tough.

Along the way, ole Frank took to more serious crimes that somebody else always took the rap for. Like the hold-up of the Kingsway Movie Theatre for the Saturday night bank deposit bag. Everybody knew he was behind it. And grand theft auto, the time he slid behind the wheel of a Jeep Cherokee at Belsano's Used Cars, and drove it off in broad daylight. Next thing we knew, he was a cop. Now he's a homicide detective. Don't ask.

I followed Tony inside. One more year had gone by in my life, and I was back in the place where I'd scored my first allowance increase. This time I had a brand new, great job to show off. Private eyes are not rolling in dough – except maybe Tango Daly, and I'm still not sure how to break that one down – and now I had a shot at lots of outside cash. Maybe Pop would ease up on the car talk. Ever since the Mercedes became mine, he'd been pressing me to trade it in on something less expensive. Pocket da change, he said, pay some bills. But like I said, the car was my one real extravagance. I wasn't getting any younger, and nice cars like that don't just fall off a turnip truck.

Likewise, the downtown highrise condo right on Lake Erie, on Lakefront Boulevard... or as Pop says, Flakefront because of all the young people. But the apartment was a necessity. No way I was moving back home like Tony did. My condo was mirrored, marbled and mine, as long as I could pay the taxes and the monthly fees, which were sixty days past due.

I rounded the corner of the house, into the front room. Pop, ever the optimist, was still sitting at the dining room table staring into an empty dish. To the right was the living room, and straight ahead the kitchen looked out onto the backyard. Pop was a retired cop, whose life now centered on mealtimes. His only other relief from my mother's CIA-grade surveillance was hanging out with former police department colleagues. They had a collective office in our basement. It housed very old cold case files over which they toiled, in hopes of solving them. So far they had an impressive record. They'd cracked two, a murder and a robbery. I handed him a sample of my new swag.

"Take a look at my business cards. Nice, huh? These are just the temporary ones, but they have the name of the TV station on them, and under my name they say News Reporter, just like I never left."

"P. J. Santini." My father tested the words, rolling them around like a mouthful of ravioli.

"Aaaaaayyyyy!" Ma dropped the meat fork into the sink and her five-foot-two-inch frame came smoking out of the kitchen, wet hands making furious passes at her apron. "What, you couldn't use your whole name? Your heritage isn't good enough, eh *principessa*? Do you hear her, Dominic?" she said to my father.

"Ma, I'm using Santini already. That's my name, I never changed it. See what you did here, Pop?" He stared at me and then at Ma, and raised a finger to say something, but nothing came out. Silence is the secret to longevity in that house.

Ma closed her eyes for the journey to that big Sunday dinner in the sky, like this new crisis had finally sucked the life's blood out of her. "That's not your name, Pommie. PJ is what you wear to bed. Where's the rest of it?"

"If you two had given me a normal name, I'd be using it, wouldn't I. Whoever heard of saddling a girl with Pompeo Jiacobbe Santini?"

"It was good enough for your poor, dear grandfather, God rest his soul." Ma said. "You should be happy your father changed Jiacobbe from a G to a J, so you'd be PJS and not PGS. Those kinds of initials stand for things like Perimeter Gunnery System or Pubertal Growth Spurt."

"What? That's not the point! My grandfather was *a guy*. I don't care how badly you wanted a boy, you got me first, and you should have made some adjustments. Why didn't you save the good name for my brother? Give *me* a name like Tony, I could live with a name like Tony. A girl with a name like mine... if I didn't already have a gun, I'd have to go out and get one."

At that, my father's mouth unhinged, and he took on my mother without moving his eyes from the plate. "By god ,Margie, da name worked. *Da girl's got balls*!"

"Oh J-M-J," Tony moaned .

"What's J-M-J? "I asked.

"Jesus, Mary and Joseph. I can't get the whole thing out anymore without somebody interruptin'. Ruins the whole effect."

"Anyway, people call me Janice, so there's your..." I mumbled, deflated, and made for the wine jug on the floor at my father's feet. It was his favorite brand: a gallon. I collapsed beside it in my good suit, and Tony handed me down a glass.

I had to give my mother credit, she was a sorceress in the kitchen. The meatballs were as good as Nonna's, and we all threw down enough to atone for whatever we should be feeling guilty about that day. It's the Italian way. If Mama ain't happy, ain't nobody happy, and she's happy when we're eating. Ten minutes after the chocolate birthday cake with coconut cream frosting went to work on my thighs, we stuffed the last of the dishes into the washer. Then when I was least expecting it, she broadsided me. "I don't care if I don't have a daughter anymore. It's alright, you owe me nothing."

"What?"

"Do I know you, well-fed lady in the suit I gave you? What's your name?"

"Oh god."

"Never mind, don't answer now. Think it over. Text me. It's poker night."

"I will *not* text you," I told her.

Without missing a beat, Ma turned to Tony. "Son, put out the flamingo."

"Okay, but what's always with the flamingo next to St. Francis on Thursday? What's goin' on?" Tony had a vested interest in that part of the yard. Plus, he was ready for any dogfight that might relieve the boredom of his job as a cable guy. "I'm not doin' it again unless you tell me."

"Okay, here's the deal, but you can't say anything to anybody, especially your father. We do a little side betting at St. Agatha's. We're running our own Executive Game, see? Tonight I feel lucky. I'm going to double my bet. When the ante goes up to twenty bucks, the flamingo goes out to let the girls know. That way they don't forget to show. Oh ho, somebody's gonna win big tonight!"

"How many sixty-year-old girls would that be?" I asked Ma, regretting ever introducing her to The Sopranos.

"A shitload."

"Ma! Are you betting twenty dollars of grocery money every week? What if you lose?"

"*Che sera sera*. Niagara falls. Anything can happen."

Pop stirred. "Aw, geeeeez." The news was on TV. I headed for the door with a take-out bag of my mother's coronary bypass special.

"No, wait," Tony had me by the arm. "Don't go. Somebody tell me how you can make a twenty-dollar cash side bet on a penny-ante church poker game!"

"You can't," I said. "I don't think."

Before I could get the car into gear, the cell phone started. It was the newsroom. Gerald Sigmund's brother, Harold, wanted me to call him, pronto. "Harold?" I asked the reporter who took the message. "Gerald and Harold? You're kidding. Can't it wait until morning?"

"I don't think so. He was pretty worked up. I wouldn't give him your number."

"Good man." I punched in Harold Sigmund's number while Sweet Boy got us home. We were still talking when the parking garage grate went up and I drove into the lower level under my condominium building. We got disconnected in the elevator to the sixth floor. While I was waiting for the signal to come back, I thought about how Lou and I had bought the apartment before the wedding. He liked the running path just outside, and the marina. I liked the restaurant next door and the showy, ridiculously slow elevator that was reminiscent of expensive department stores.

I poured some Chianti, kicked off my shoes and called Harold back. "So what you're saying is that you don't trust the cops."

"Sure I do. I just want to get into Siggy's apartment and have my own private look-see. If he isn't back by tomorrow night, the police are going to treat him as a missing person and they'll be all over it."

"Don't you *want* them to be all over it?"

"Sure I do."

"And you want me, a humble reporter, a private investigator who knows nothing about this, to take you inside your own brother's place. Shouldn't it be the other way around?"

"I'd rather not talk about it over the phone," he said. "I want to go in on behalf of the family, just to see if everything looks okay. You're the logical person to do this, since you took over his job. But I don't have a key, uh, anymore."

"Goodbye, Harold." It wasn't his words, it was the soft, insinuating monotone that sounded so unnatural it made the hairs stand up on my arms.

"No, wait. I can tell you where to get it. It's better if you get it."

Something else about this sounded undesirable, maybe everything, but I had to ask. "Okay, I'll bite. Where's your key?"

"Honey's got it, Siggy's girlfriend. She's a dancer."

"You mean like a ballerina?" I asked.

"I mean like a stripper. Honey Summer. She works at My Apartment over on Wiley, off Clinton. She'll give it to you if you tell her you need to check on notes Siggy made for a story he was working on." Nothing wrong here. Except that a man's own brother has to sneak into his home, doesn't dare ask for a key, and I have to lie to get it from a bubble dancer. It had all the appeal of a train wreck. Which was why I couldn't resist it.

Next morning, I rolled out of bed in a pretty good mood, and pulled the draperies back to look through the floor-to-ceiling bedroom windows at another white-hot Friday. Waiters on the restaurant patio at ground level were tucking fluttering napkins under plates, while an independently wealthy Ralph Lauren ad was easing his thirty-foot sailboat out of the marina. Or maybe, this being Buffalo, he was ripping it off while I was watching.

I mulled over the perfect outfit to wear to see Honey Summer at the strip joint. To blend in, I squeezed Ma's Fettuccini Alfredo into my skinny jeans – as opposed to the currently better-fitting fat jeans – and put on a skintight pink sleeveless pajama top that said *Sweet Enough* in sparkly glitter. I hoped Honey wouldn't take off points because my hot pink heels were genuine Miu Miu.

Traffic on Clinton was moving okay, going east out of downtown. The My Apartment club lurked on a street called Norseman. Norseman ran for two blocks, between Clinton and a dead end. The only other businesses were a chop shop and a grocery with bars on the windows. Hence, my decision to forego the back lot and leave the car out front, where I could keep an eye on it. By the time I parked, the jeans had cut off circulation from the knees down. I swung out and literally fell off my shoes. In a part of town that places a high value on drunk and disorderly, this kind of behavior could only enhance my resume', so I decided not to worry about it. Besides, the street was deserted.

Inside, the place had a coat of fresh paint. I think. The light was pretty dim. The walls were dark purple. There were a few tables and chairs, and a bar ran the length of the wall to the left of the stage. On the right side, there was a curtained door leading to the back. Mostly the big room had cushy, worn sofas covered in a splotchy, modern purple-and-white print.

"Hey doll, how long you been missin' from the convent? You can't dance here lookin' like that. Get your ass in the back and jack up your standards." He had to be the bouncer. Thick neck, black polyester jacket that reeked of cigarettes and sweat, and a .45-calibre bulge where everybody else was wearing a BlackBerry. Nice to know that at ten in the morning, rested, lipsticked and trashy, I'd been rejected as an exotic gyrator in a sleezy dive.

"No shit, Einstein. Thanks for the tip. Maaco's on the way with the makeup," I shot back, and reached into my purse for a Hershey bar. Do not aggravate me in the morning. I don't care how big, how mean, how dumb you are, aggravation leads to chocolate and then into dangerous territory. "I need to talk to Honey. I'm a pal." He didn't leave right away. He thought about it for a second, struggled to fake thought a second longer, then went to get her behind the stage. I took that time to peruse the sofas, looking for the repetition in the pattern, and gagged when I realized the fabric wasn't patterned in white, it was stained.

A song made up mostly of four-letter words and a bass guitar kicked in. When Honey finally negotiated the steps onto the platform and stood up in her five-inch silver stilettos, I had to admit she had a traffic-stopping chassis. Siggy knew how to pick 'em. She ignored me, doing some sort of early morning Buddhist meditation with the pole. Then she slid down it very fast, courageously risking spontaneous combustion in her crotch.

She crawled on all fours to my end of the stage, tossed her head around so that her regulation waist-length blonde, wavy mane caught the rotating blue lights, and pursed her lips. She executed a Downward Facing Dog, and murmured, "Yeah?" Honey was already high. I hoped I could get past her before it wore off, so I motor-mouthed it:

"Hi there! I don't know if you remember me, I'm really in a huge hurry. I'm PJ Santini, and I've taken over Gerald Sigmund's job while he's away. He was working on a story and I really, really need his notes on that. They're in his apartment, it's really important and it's an emergency. Could you please lend me the key, and I promise to bring it right back?"

Her front stopped moving, but her back kept going, like when they cut the head off a snake on Discovery Channel. "Ummmm, who are you?" Dilated pupils trying to focus, and not having much luck at it.

"I'm Janice, Siggy's journalist friend. I just need very quickly to get into his apartment to pick up my notes on a news story, okay? Just tell me where your bag is and I'll be gone and back really fast. I'm double-parked, too."

She frowned. "Ummmmm, it's the pink one. Shiny."

"Thanks, be right back." I skipped like a schoolgirl past the gorilla and found the dressing room. Seedy wouldn't be the right word... it has seed in it, something that has a rat's ass of a chance of developing into something productive. More girls, and almost-girls, were lounging on old chewed-up PVC lawn chairs, five or six of them. They were in various stages of painting, pasting and hormone therapy. I hadn't expected that, and hadn't worked up more of a cover story. They weren't like Honey, most were lucid and wary. I prayed I could get in and out fast.

"What're you looking for?" the one in the black feather boa asked.

"Honey's lending me something. Said to get it out of her pink bag. Where's the bag?"

"What do you want to get out of it?" Now the others had stopped fiddling with their bits.

"Just the keys, just for a minute."

A group representative in a red chicken feather G-string and a really flattering Dolly Parton wig said, "You just want to have a look at her personal property, no big thing? Why, you a narc? Or maybe somethin' else."

"No, no, of course not, not a narc, not anything." Daly says they can always smell your fear. So I smiled big. Which probably told them I was scared shitless. "She gave me permission. Hey, here's an idea, *you* get her bag and *you* reach in and hand me the keys, okay? I don't know what else is in there, and I don't care." All this was taking too much time. Honey could go on break and come back in, any minute... unless she'd soldered herself to the pole by now.

The pussy posse had closed ranks, blocking my view of the door. I struggled to keep my eyes from bouncing all over the room in a panic, as I tried calculating the distance. Then the one with the boa yelled huskily, "Damian baby, come on in here! Hustle!" She turned to the others. "Things ain't addin' up, past few weeks. Information's scarce, am I right?"

Nice going, PJ Now the chills are starting. You're stuck in a windowless cell, with Satan's sisters and a Neanderthal between you and freedom. You want a gunfight in here? How many of them are carrying, besides the knuckle dragger and you? Guns. Or worse, knives. I hate knives. All my blood must have rushed to my vital organs, because I was so cold my teeth were chattering. "Ladies, I'm just a reporter and..."

"*A reporter*?" A muscular six-footer in a lemon-yellow corset and Elvira wig pushed through the group and lunged, sinking his fingers into the sides of my throat with enough force to slam me off my feet into the full length mirror nailed to the wall. It shattered and I shrieked. I reached back and tried to pry off a big piece of glass before they got the same idea, but nothing came loose. His grip was tightening, cutting off my air. He had me pinned with only one hand, but it was at the end of an arm so long there was no way I could reach his body.

I thought about kicking his nuts up into his nostrils, but he was angled sideways and looked real comfortable with it. While he was scrubbing my scalp against the broken glass, grating it like cheese, the pressure was building in my face, and I pictured it swollen and purple with blood spurting out my ears. "What *kinda* story you workin' on, sweetheart? Mysteries uh love? What *kinda* love you *want*?" Concentrating wasn't easy. Currents of pain were pumping spastic jerks into my fingers, and I really hoped he didn't think I was flipping him off. Or wanting something special.

"You like pain?" Elvira asked. "Look like she ready for an education. Look like she ready for a test drive." He squashed his nose against mine. I could smell the chemical slipperiness of the thick, oily makeup that had collected in his sweaty pock marks, and around his beard. I didn't want that to be my last memory of life on this planet. "*Damian!*"

his voice deepened, "*Getcher ass in here!* I'm gonna waste you, bitch. But first, I'm gonna give you somethin' to remember."

My purse had slipped off my shoulder about five heart attacks ago, but since I never was big on keeping my gun in anything that could be taken away from me, I had it holstered on my ankle. I'd often wondered if I could really pull the trigger on another human being. Absofuckinlutely. "Damian!" I croaked too, with the air I had left, just to confuse them and buy a few seconds. I needed to work my leg up and pull the Sig out from under my jeans, the tight ones that I could barely bend in to drive. I was almost there, when Honey appeared in the doorway and the whole scene froze.

"What's the matter?" she babytalked. "Damian's taking a smoke break."

Elvira let me drop to the floor, and everybody started talking at once. "She's a narc...wanted your bag...vice or somethin' ...let the bitch ...takin' chances..." All I could think, while I was crawling around in broken glass, sputtering and hacking through windpipe spasms, was that I had about ten seconds to get myself up to a standing position. Your hunter sees you're wounded, you can say goodnight.

Honey sighed deeply and toddled over to the big, glossy strawberry plastic duffle that had been lying four feet away from me the whole time. She squatted and dug into the inside pocket. Out came a key ring, hooked onto the iridescent half-inch fuchsia claw of her middle finger. She dangled it at me. I was upright just in time.

"Good girl," I said, snatching it like it was the last cannoli before Lent. Every painful footstep drove razor-sharp fragments deeper into my scalp, and drew more blood. The goon Damian was loitering at the front door. When he saw me, he straightened up and exhaled smoke. His pea-sized brain was mesmerized by the dark red liquid snaking around my neck. It had reached the *Sweet Enough* on my t-shirt, pooling in a big wet patch that molded stickily to my chest. He straightened and looked real interested. I whipped around toward the car.

The car. It was gone. Sweet Boy was gone! How could I have been so stupid, to leave him here with no protection in a neighborhood like this? He had no LoJack, no GPS emergency service because I hadn't had the money to keep it going when it lapsed two months ago, and no security system. No, no, no! I got out my cell phone and galloped toward Clinton. Please, *please* let it work. Iroquois Investigations has a special 800 number reserved for operatives' emergencies. Calls go directly to Tango Daly.

"Operations," Daly answered on the third ring.

"Help! Help!" I gasped, yanking my Miu Miu's out of the pavement cracks. "I've been cut by a six-foot tranny in a strip joint where lap dances come without Kleenex! They took Sweet Boy from out front! He's gone and I've got no ride. I'm bleeding. They think I'm a narc and they want to kill me! Kill me! Tango, help!"

"Who is this?"

"That is... not... funny."

"Okay, Janice, it's going to be okay. Tell me how badly you're hurt and exactly where you are."

Eleven minutes later, Daly screeched to a stop at Clinton and Why Me, and I jumped in.

"What kind of message do you think this nice, understated black BMW 700 series pimpmobile with tinted windows, dual exhausts and twelve antennas might be sending to these people about me?" I asked.

"Only a woman would do a transportation critique at a time like this. It's telling them that it is unacceptable that they stood by and watched a homie boost your Sweet Boy right in front of the club, while you were getting fucked up inside. It's telling them you've got friends. Very angry friends of a certain, shall we say, para-legitimate persuasion, who don't appreciate what has taken place here, and will not forget it."

Daly's knuckles were absolutely white on the steering wheel, his fingers straightening and flexing as he drove. He was exerting real effort to stay cool. I'd never seen him like that.

He spoke in a forceful monotone. "Here's what we're going to do. We're going to the ER first, in case you need stitches, and definitely for pain meds, that must hurt like hell. Then to the police station, so they can get a good look at you and take the report. I already talked to Kielbasa, they're waiting." Leon Kielbasa was my friend from way back, a cop who normally worked homicides. One of the good guys, which was probably why he was still a sergeant. Leon was one of the smartest decisions I never made. Never dated, never even went to a dance together, still friends who never fight. See how that works?

"Thanks for coming to get me, Tango. I really mean it." I stifled a sob with the back of my hand. The palm was all cut up.

"I know you do, honey," his voice softened. "It's okay." Different silk shirt, different Italian slacks, same classy guy. His fingers were resting on the back of my neck where blood had congealed. I was exhausted. The adrenaline rush was over, and I felt safe enough to cry in relief that I'd come out alive. "I was really freaked. But listen, it's not bleeding so much now, and my head's numb. Wouldn't it be okay if I cleaned up before we go over to the Precinct? I don't want them to see me like this. Plus, assault charges will never fly, because there'll never be any witnesses. Please?"

"Doesn't matter. Got to get this one on the books. Could be important later. From what you said, they're worried about a lot more than apartment keys. If it's a narcotics thing and it's business, it's more than just a few fry sticks."

Fry sticks aren't as bigtime as crack or crystal meth, but they aren't good for you, either. They're marijuana cigarettes dipped in formaldehyde, or sometimes PCP. Big sellers with the underage crowd. You'd have to be a pretty stupid to prefer that to a Golden – that's Buffalo-speak, for a Molson. "And," Daly said, "you do have pieces of glass in your head, as hard as your head happens to be. I can see them from here."

The emergency room took three whole hours. When I came out, I had four stitches and a lovely bandage that went around my head and under my chin, and looked like the Spirit of '76. Daly made me leave it on at the police station while Kielbasa filled out the reports. When I got home, it was going to come off if I had to *chew* it off. He walked me to the front of my condo building and we eased into the elevator.

"You're on your honor," he said on the way up. "Say you'll stay home." Because I'm a below average liar, I kept my mouth shut and simply nodded yes. He helped me onto the bed without a single wisecrack, slipped me a nice full-contact smooch and tiptoed out. I listened for the door to close and the deadbolt to click home. If you can't trust Tango Daly with a key, who can you trust? On the other hand, I had no intention of staying in. I made a mental note to work out the whole reciprocal honor issue at a later date.

Two minutes later, I'd found a bag of Goldfish crackers to jump-start my thought process, as I rummaged for a chiffon scarf to wrap around my neck. It would camouflage Elvira's beet-colored fingerprints, and a hat would take care of the bandage. I'd earned the right to use Honey's key to Gerald Sigmund's apartment and I was going to use it, right now.

THREE

FORTUNATELY, THE AUTO insurance on Sweet Boy hadn't lapsed along with everything else in my life. While I was waiting for the company to send over a loaner, I buffed up and tried not to think about where my wonderful car could be by now, or who'd had the gall to steal it. It was demoralizing, like being punched in the stomach. Avoiding the hamburger on the back of my head, I showered off the blood and the fear, and changed into fresh jeans and a nice, loose top to cover something of new importance... an elastic belly band holster, my favorite, the one with the little pink ribbon bow. I wanted the gun above my waist, where I could reach it better. Plus, I wasn't supposed to bend down because of the bleeding.

The loaner was waiting at the curb. It was small and green, much too army surplus to get attached to – or to steal. Who'd do five years for a toad like this? No doubt it would be an easy fill-up, Pop would like that. But it was so ugly I'd have to sneak up on the pump. Actually, it reminded me of my first car, a manual transmission Chevy Biscayne that Pop had driven first. No carpet, no tinted windows, and of course no air conditioning. The whole car got so hot on long trips, Ma would put an entire dinner... beef and potatoes... in foil under the hood. By the time we stopped for the night, dinner was ready.

Gerald Sigmund lived at 1361 Leonardo, Building C, off Hertel Avenue. Basically, an address surrounded by Mediterraneans. I prayed he was feeling gut-wrenching Italian guilt-by-osmosis, for putting me through this. His brother Harold and I had agreed to meet in the lobby at four. I arrived at 3:45 P.M., to have time to drive around back and park where I could see the lot entrance. Watching Harold pull up, studying the way he handled his car, would tell me something about the man. When he said he'd be driving a silver 2006 Mercedes E-class, I felt a pang of anxiety over Sweet Boy. I hoped he was being treated well.

3:49 P.M. My head was killing me; but if I took pain pills I wouldn't be able to drive. Or shoot straight. Or say my name.

At exactly ten minutes to four, Harold eased into the lot, taking care not to high-center his ride on the elevated pavement. He didn't go right to a space. He drove around, twice. Finally, he parked and killed the engine. Polished shoes and grey summer-weight wool came out first. A pretty rich set-up for an electronics store computer repair technician. Daly had run a backgrounder on him. Okay, maybe the high-buck car was a lease, but what about the clothes? He had expensive tastes. He looked around, scanned the environment, locked up and disappeared inside. On the way in, I took down 007's plate number, just for laughs.

"Right on time," I said behind him, and he jumped half a foot. He'd been watching through the front lobby window, obviously expecting me to be driving something he hadn't seen in the lot. He didn't look a thing like his brother. Siggy was average height, blond, thin and 39. Harold was 43, short, with a shiny dome surrounded by salt-and-pepper curls, and a belly. But the biggest difference was in the eyes: Siggy's were knowing. Harold's were watchful.

Siggy's apartment was on the third floor. I turned the key that may or may not have been Harold's before Honey got it and I wangled it out of her, and the deadbolt slid open. But I wasn't going to be the one to turn the knob. It would've been nice to stop action and ask the judges for a ruling on breaking and entering, but when it comes to B&E I prefer to leave judges out of it. "After you," I told Harold. Was I a bad person for thinking that if shots rang out, Harold could field the first volley? After all, he *was* family.

No sordid surprises in the living room. In fact, it looked nice, what they call eclectic. Clean lines, nothing tacky. But nothing like Siggy, either. I asked Harold if it looked the same as before, and when was the last time he'd been there.

"Looks pretty much the same. Honey wasn't much of a decorator. Norbert does it for a living." Harold was going through the kitchen drawers. He found a Phillips head screwdriver and started lifting the vent covers off the air ducts.

"Excuse me? Norbert who?" I asked him.

"Norbert Dojka. Siggy's latest flame is of the male persuasion. Boy, Honey sure was pissed. Hurt, actually. Norbert's the head window dresser at Hartwig's. Never covers the window when he works, he likes it when people watch. Takes extra time smoothing down the wrinkles, if you know what I mean. Gets a discount on clothes, too. His are a lot nicer than Honey's." Harold looked in the dishwasher, then in the refrigerator and the smell of dead greenery wafted across the room. Red wine had crystallized in a stem glass in the sink.

"So Honey doesn't live here. Why did you lend her your key?"

"She needed to pick up something from before." He pulled the plastic trash can out from under the sink. Empty, no liner.

"And she didn't want to run into Siggy's new sweetie?"

"Bingo."

"Know what she wanted?"

"Nope." He moved to the living room, and was taking the couch apart when I asked him again what he was looking for. "Nothing," he said. "Anything."

Siggy had an upscale sound system and a 52" top-of-the-line flat screen HDTV. But no computer. A working reporter who wasn't in the office every day would have to have a computer at home. At least a laptop. This looked like the first clue that he really had taken off on his own.

I followed Harold into the bedroom. Everything looked tidy and, well, like a department store window. A burled wood men's jewelry box on the shelf of an open armoire held neatly arranged cufflinks and watches. The king size bed was made. Two lightweight waffled cotton spa bathrobes lay folded and ready at the bottom. The toes of twin pairs of hotel slippers peeked out exactly one-and-a-half inches from under the dust ruffle.

In the bathroom, two electric toothbrushes were fully charged. If a guy were going to go away – or run away – he'd at least take his toothbrush. And something to wear. In the walk-in closet off the bathroom, only a couple of hangers were empty. Everything seemed to be in order, including the kimonos and the Vera Wangs.

"Harold, do you have any idea where Siggy is? Do you know if he packed some clothes? Is anything missing?"

"Hard to say." I didn't appreciate that he was ignoring me completely. He pulled open a drawer, and there was more lingerie than Victoria's Secret. Good stuff that made me jealous.

"Looks like Honey didn't take it all," I said.

"Check the size. I'd say it's Norbert's." He dug out a two hundred dollar receipt from a shop called Fancy's Pants, and left me standing by the dresser. That was the last straw.

"Okay Columbo, just a damn minute. What the hell's going on? What's your agenda?" I yanked off the scarf to expose my nasty purple neck. I jerked off the hat and turned around so he could get an eyeful of the bloody bandage.

"Your brother's disappeared. I got the bejesus pounded out of me today at Honey's hellhole, which you knew all about when you sent me over. My car's been stolen. And an emergency room intern Betsy Rossed all over the back of my head – several minutes, I might add, before the anesthetic kicked in."

When I heard myself saying it, I got *really* mad. "I poured out my life story to a duty room full of cops who only wanted to know where transvestite bubble dancers stash their packages. All to get your damn key. Tell me what's going on, right now, or I'm taking all of this back to the Precinct."

I hoped he wouldn't call my bluff, because there was nothing here... no guns, no drugs, nothing to tell the police. And I probably did break and enter. But Harold was the only link to what had happened to me at My Apartment, and I had to know.

He acted insulted I would even suggest he was playing me for a sucker. "I'm sorry," he said, "I didn't know about all of that. I was just worried that something was wrong with my brother. Knowing him, anything is possible. But everything looks fine. It's just that Norbert hasn't been answering the phone." The same thought flashed across our minds at the same time. Voice mail. He got to the phone before I did, and hit Play. Nothing but nine hang-ups.

"Listen, I've taken enough of your time," he said, checking his watch. "I'll get right to the point. I'd like to hire you to find my brother. And I'll be needing his personal papers, to pay his bills. They're not here, so maybe they're in your office."

"That's very flattering, Harold, but after what happened at My Apartment, I'd say finding him is definitely what the cops are for. As for his papers, I don't have them." He could just include me out of that whole thing.

"But you're the logical person to do this. You haven't seen him in years, so you have no preconceptions. And after all, you *are* working in his office now."

"Yeah, you said that yesterday, and look what happened today. No thanks."

"I have the money, PJ. Cash. I'll pay you double."

"I'll call Iroquois Investigations so we can draw up the contract."

"Good. Then I'll be needing that key back."

"No can do, Harold. All due respect, it doesn't have your name on it. I got it from Honey Summer and I have to get it back to her... somehow." Air dropping it would be good. Or FedEx. Should I tell them about Damian?

As we left, and in my new capacity as Mata Hari, I took an extra couple of minutes to fish around in Siggy's refrigerator to make sure we hadn't overlooked any plastic bags of dope sunk into mayonnaise jars, or olives stuffed with .22 rounds. I didn't find anything; but I couldn't shake the feeling that the answer was right under my nose.

On the way home, I stopped at a hardware store on Hertel and had them rip off a copy of the key, you know, in case Honey ever lost hers. What are friends for? Then I called Daly, and told him where I'd been. He wasn't happy. I filled him in on Harold... the expensive threads, the methodical search of his brother's apartment, and the fact that he didn't seem as worried about Siggy as he ought to be. I told him Siggy had thrown over his girlfriend for a guy who made a living diddling mannequins in front of anybody who would stop and watch.

When I got to the cash part, Daly said to take the case. In the morning I planned to pop in Daly's office and pick up the papers, then meet Harold so he could make a two thousand dollar non-refundable donation to my MasterCard.

By now it was past evening rush hour. I caught Raycroft and headed home to take medicine and climb into bed. Treating the Toad to underground parking seemed like a waste of perfectly good underground parking, but I did it anyway. When the elevator came to a stop on the sixth floor, it nearly brought me to my knees. The doctor said that might happen. I tilted through the front door and was halfway to the bedroom, when my nose started twitching like a rabbit. I was hallucinating the thing I needed most... Chinese take-out. And then I saw him, watching from the easy chair by the couch.

"What're you doing here?" I asked Daly. "The food's piping hot... how'd you even know when I'd be home?" He was looking very domestic, dishing up egg drop soup and fried rice from Wei-To-Go. Everything was on the coffee table.

"You're a bad girl. You should check your rearview more often. No, wait. I'll do that for you." He didn't get up. He wasn't impressed that I'd lied about staying home. I stepped out of my shoes, and used the last of my strength to knock down a Percocet and un-Velcro my belly band holster. "I didn't exactly know I was going back out, um, when you left. I sort of decided after. Sorry. It's just that I had the key..." I put the Sig on the table and plopped down on the couch. "Good ole Daisy, I almost had to use her today."

Daly slid beside me, but he still wasn't smiling. "My gun has a name, too. Have you met?"

The pill was kicking in. "Oh, you mean the Howitzer?" I said dreamily. He'd forgiven me. He'd kept an eye on me, after all. And he did smell good, and he made me feel safe. Maybe I wasn't so tired.

"You wouldn't," I whispered into his neck.

"I wouldn't? No, you're right, not tonight. I just wanted to see how you're doing. I'm here to feed you and tuck you in, though god knows why. When you're actually asleep, I'll leave."

"But I won't be able to go to sleep now," I said, pivoting to shovel General Tso's chicken into my mouth. "I'll like having you here." In the morning I'd realize what I'd said tonight, and pound my head against a

mirror until the front matched the back. But for now, I couldn't help it. I leaned into him, and he put his arms around me.

And then, just when I thought he was going to tell me this case was too dangerous, he said, "I know you're not going to drop it. So the next thing you have to do is talk to Honey again."

Two thousand dollars can do a lot for a girl's confidence. The next morning Daly let me keep Harold's deposit as an advance on operating expenses, and I became more optimistic that Gerald Sigmund would turn up. I imagined him and Norbert Dojka reclining in flowery orchid rayon kimonos against a backdrop of exotic palm trees, sipping from glasses of pink foam with crepe paper umbrellas sticking out the top. Siggy turns to Norbert, who looks just like Patrick Dempsey, and says, "Let's give PJ a call, so she won't worry."

Harold was not exactly churning out information, as he ordered breakfast and handed over the cash. See, his job would be to give me as many facts as possible, so that I could actually do *my* job, but that wasn't happening. We were sitting in an Omelet's, a Mom-and-Popish chain of diners that serve nothing but good ole American hamburgers, and eggs fifty ways. They all look exactly alike: a counter in the front, booths on the side, mirror on the wall behind the last booth, by the emergency exit. Daly had taught me to sit in the back. Privacy and security, he said. The back wasn't available, so I picked a booth where I could watch through the mirror.

I had to drag the information out of Harold. When did he last see Siggy? Last Monday, the day before he evaporated. He act weird? No weirder than usual. Harold still wanted his key back, and I still said no. I asked who Siggy's friends were.

"Siggy has no friends," he said. I found that hard to believe. His overall standards were lower than a snake's belly, so that left room for just about everybody. "There is one guy. George. He's a personal trainer."

"George have a last name?"

"Cabral. Portuguese. At Jock's Gym, over on Vanguard." This being Saturday, I thought there was a good chance of sighting Cabral in his natural habitat. It was a short ride, Jock's Gym was in the same neighborhood as Omelet's.

Space is at a premium in decent parts of Buffalo. This wasn't one of them, so the gym was the size of HSBC Arena. I pulled into the side lot and didn't lock the Toad, then a pang of guilt sent me back... after all, he had gotten me this far. The gym's front door was open, and floor fans were rustling the weight lifting diagrams taped to the far wall. I winced at all the mirrors on the side walls, and took two steps back. In the middle, sweaty guys of every description were bench pressing and skipping rope, comparing six-packs under bright florescent lights.

Without my Sweet Enough tee, I was being completely ignored. "George!" I hollered at the only likely candidate. He waited until his client took a break.

"Hey, hon, what's up?" George's thick widow's peak came up to my boobs. He was built compact and low to the ground, like a bulldog. They even had the same underbite. And ears.

"My name's PJ Santini. I'm looking for Gerald Sigmund. Thought you might know where he is."

"Why would I know?"

"You're a friend of his."

"Ain't seen him in weeks. He owes me money."

"Mind if I ask what for?"

"It's personal," Cabral said. Why would Siggy, who was living very comfortably, owe a guy like Cabral? I should have pushed him on that, but the goddamn mirrors were closing in. I handed him my card and said to call if he heard anything. As I went out the front, I caught Cabral's reflection hustling right past his client, vanishing through the papered-over door in the back wall.

I knew I should get in touch with Honey and meet her someplace, like Daly said, but I just couldn't do it, not yet. I told myself – and it didn't take much convincing – that I ought to put in an appearance at the TV station. The sad truth is that if you don't show up, they don't keep cutting the checks. Swinging into my employee parking space without Sweet Boy, I felt like I was cheating on him with the Toad. Not a word from the cops on his whereabouts, either. I was feeling well enough to get really, really mad about that.

I hit the wall switch and left the lights to power up while I ran over to Eccola's Grocery for cleaning supplies. I'd need gloves. That was another thing. My wigs, gummy bears and a brand new box of latex gloves were still in the trunk of the SLK. Somebody was going to have a good time.

I wheeled the cart to the cleaning products aisle and rounded up paper towels and, I'm sorry to say, thick yellow gloves, the kind Ma made me wear when I was a kid and had to help her clean the oven. I dreaded this beyond all reason. She always did it early in the day, so the oven wasn't stinky by dinnertime. When I was eleven, I woke up one lovely summer morning, got a whiff of Easy-Off, and jumped out the bedroom window. I lost my grip on a tree branch, and wound up in the ER with a broken wrist. That got me out of cleaning until it healed. It was worth it.

Next down the aisle, I found a bottle of Mr. Clean on steroids. He said he was up for the job, and since I was looking for a man I could trust, I told him to climb in. On the way out, I swung by the personal products and snagged a box of condoms, size large, on sale with an expiration date of next month. Who says I'm not optimistic? I lined up to check out.

"Janice Santini, as I live and breathe, over here!" Antje Pooler was exactly what I didn't need, so I fiddled with my cell and pretended not to hear. "Janice! Come over!"

Antje has run the express register at Eccola's since her husband Charlie lost his job at the windshield wiper plant, and skipped town. When their kid Teeter, who graduated with me, went to Michigan to play AA hockey, Charlie hitched up the Airstream to his Olds, dropped Teeter off in Saginaw and just kept on going. This left her with no money and nothing to do. So she became an information specialist, with Eccola's as her headquarters. Everybody knows, if you want to spread news fast you can telephone, telegraph or tell Antje. She pulled my cart into her lane and started working it over.

"Well now, let's see what you've brought me today. Paper towels, okay... Mr. Clean, always a choice... latex gloves, hmm... rubbers? Somebody must have left them in the cart."

"That would be me," I said.

"But what on earth would *you* want them for?" she asked, genuinely mystified that I might have a use for them.

My face was getting red, I could feel the heat. "Same thing everybody wants them for, Mrs. Pooler." She ran the box across the scanner, but it didn't work. She tried again. "Forget it," I whispered.

But Mrs. Pooler was on a mission. She flipped the switch under the counter and the big yellow light on the *Express Lane 10 Items Or Less* sign started flashing and bing-bonging. It probably also alerted the cops, my mother and the Buffalo News. Spanky Cohn, the store manager had been taking it all in.

"Are you sure these rubbers are the ones you want?" he asked. "I'm not getting good reports about 'em. If I knew who they're for, I could get you his favorite. There's no such thing as a regular man, y' know."

"Yeah, I'm getting *that* picture," I said.

"It's alright, dear, you can tell us," Antje said, hiking up her sleeve and whipping the pen off her ear.

I was mortified. "Forget it! Ring up everything else, and nobody'll get hurt!"

"Just charge her four-fifty," Spanky said, like it didn't much matter, their probably not being used anyway.

Before the day was out, every one of Ma's friends would be inking a big red question mark across my yearbook picture.

While I was gone, somebody dropped a goofy pink *While You Were Comatose* slip on the stack of files on my desk. It said *Call Vicky...or else!* Oh my god, I was a terrible friend. Yesterday she'd phoned the house, the office, my cell, everywhere. But if I'd let her hear my voice after what happened at My Apartment, she would have wangled every last detail out of me. So I did the chicken thing and didn't talk until I was ready.

"*Balducci's Love Your Dog*, ya got Vicky here... hold still, dammit, we got five more days together, get over it!" Vicky, whose real name is

Filomena, owns *Love Your Dog*, a combination canine day spa, gourmet restaurant and doggy hotel. I could hardly hear her, for all the yapping.

"Somebody ripped off my car yesterday," I said. "You have a spare Rottweiler?"

"Coincidentally, I do. Like me, he's on a diet and pissed off enough to go out and rip up park benches. But to find a car, you need a bloodhound." No joke. Last winter the Rubins boarded their prize-

winning bloodhound, Sherlock, for eight days while they were in Bermuda. Vicky put him to work for Daly and me. Before the Rubins got their first sunburn, Sherlock had nailed bank robber Martin Chaminsky, just from the smell of his Jockeys. He'd messed them when the teller, who turned out to be his fifth grade teacher, shoved the hold-up note back with a big red C+ on it. She wagged her finger at his ski mask, "How many times do I have to tell you, Marty, it's not *gimme*, it's *give me*."

"Oh yeah? *Now* who's the critic, Mrs. Roberts!" Martin shrieked as he bent over and cut a weather-changing shart. Next day, a kid found his shorts in a dumpster three blocks down, and the bloodhound took over from there. Iroquois Investigations took credit for tracking down Chaminsky. Certain members of the police force, working night and day on that case, never got over it. Like Officer Wolenski. Hence, Sweet Boy's parking ticket.

"Come with me to Ma's, tomorrow," I told Vicky. "Sundays, nobody diets. On the way over, we need to talk to a drugged-up stripper. Maybe we can catch her in a K-hole, and she'll accidentally tell the truth."

"Oh cool, is that like a pothole?"

"Not exactly. I have a feeling a nasty item called Special K is her hallucinogen of choice. When you fall into a K-hole, you're toast until further notice."

Back in my office, the lights still weren't fully on, but the computer screen was bright, so I checked for email – mine, Siggy's, anybody's.

My Inbox, of course, had zero. Siggy's was bulging. A lot was internal newsroom stuff, Read-Me's to anybody in the building with a pulse. I dumped those, and printed out the personal ones.

Over by the door, a vintage *AN-AmeriNews* wire service machine sprang to life. So Siggy had a soft spot for nostalgia. Bigger stations don't use these anymore, since everything's on computer. The machines are slow and noisy like a huge typewriter, and rattle so hard they almost move across the floor. But they're dependable. A computer might crash; the machine hardly ever does.

While the emails were coming off the laser jet, I tore off a long roll of *AN-AmeriNews* wire copy and scanned the local Weekly News Wrap-Up, just for old times sake. That reminded me, in order to report the news of the day I ought to be paying actual attention to it. So I went back to the computer and clicked on *Wires.Priority.Local.Weekly*, where I could copy and paste all the latest stories I needed into my own files. I didn't want to spend a lot of time on that on a Saturday, so I printed them out. That way, I could take them with me and look at everything at home – Siggy's private emails, the online news printout and the old-fashioned stuff off the machine. Maybe with a nice glass of wine, and leftover Chinese. Hershey's almond kisses for dessert.

Next, I did a drawer check. The center one was uninteresting. Paper clips, Hilighters, felt tip pens, a calculator, and the girls' names that I'd pulled out of the trash. The three drawers on the left held square padded envelopes and plain paper. Very un-Siggylike, way too orderly. Where were the sniffing glue and blow-up dolls? On the other side, the two lower drawers were packed with wire copy ripped off the machine. It was really strange – every story had the exact same subject line, the same slug: *Costa Rican drug bust*. But the dates went back more than two years. No story has the same slug for that long. The wording looked identical, too. So I piled all of it with the Stickies onto my purse.

Next, I upended the Eccola's bag onto the desktop, and fixed a High Noon stare at the top right drawer. It would be no match for my knife. Maneuvering a sharp object in floppy kitchen gloves is not an exact science, and once I got the hang of it things moved right along.

The blade chipped away at the dried goo between the desk and the drawer. Black slivers flew up and I had to spit one out. *Oh hell, put some muscle into it.* I gave it enough to pop it open. The pungent odor was a lot like week-old Indian take-out mixed with tobacco. I finessed the drawer two more inches, then two more. A towel was soaked with thick, dark liquid. I squeezed my eyes shut and eased it the rest of the way. Something shiny was sitting on top. I covered my mouth and leaned in. It was gold. Looked almost like a heavy class ring, with lots of busywork. In the middle was the universal male ball-and-arrow symbol, Mars' mythological shield and spear.

The ring had a long, thin roll of stained paper towel shoved through it... paper towel with a neatly manicured nail, half moon and all. When my mind processed that this was somebody's finger, my tank emptied... I threw up all over it. Then I just barely made it to the waste basket for round two. Now, I am not a woman who spits up like a dainty coed at a frat party. When I hurl, you can hear it a block away. The whole weekend crew was lined up at the door, but only the tape editor had the guts to poke his head in. "Is it the toilet again?" he asked. "Do we need the plunger?"

I ignored that, and went back for another look. Somebody brought a dripping wet paper towel so I could clean off my face. When I saw that, I barfed on my chair. *Do not sit in it, for god's sake, that would not be good.*

My first rambling phone call went out to Leon Kielbasa at the police station. Then to Tango Daly. As usual, Daly got there first.

"Why is it that where there's blood, there's Janice?" He gave me a squeeze, and I stomped hard on his foot. "But how can we tell it's blood, with diner food hurled all over it?"

"You are soooo going to pay for that. One lousy cinnamon roll didn't hold me. Plus, you can't meet a client in a diner and not eat," I said, defending breakfast with Harold. "Do you think the finger is Siggy's? This is his office."

"That doesn't necessarily give him ownership rights."

By the time Officer Kielbasa arrived, the crowd had multiplied. He radioed it in, then he told everybody they'd have to back off and clear the entire hallway, seeing as how he would have liked to close the door to the apparent crime scene, but *a certain person* had barfed all over the office, and he needed to let in some air or he was going to pass out.

"Wait, I think I have a clue," Daly said, holding up the box of condoms and examining it against the light. "Unopened. This must be what happens when a guy forgets to wear protection. Pretty stiff penalty."

"The condoms are mine," I confessed.

"That's what I meant." Daly said.

"Smartass."

An uncomfortable hour passed, and just when I saw hope for getting out of there, who should darken the doorstep but homicide detective and Christmas angel thief Frank Longoria. The brim of the theatrical Eliot Ness hat he wore everywhere, hopefully to cover up a large, pus-filled carbuncle, sank his eyes into shadow. He asked a lot of questions. He played with his fingernails. He had everybody, including Daly and me, fingerprinted. Well *naturally* my prints were going to be all over my own office. Why would I plant a finger in my own drawer, and then call the cops? Frank must have lingered too long over the spray paint.

People began showing up who don't even work weekends. Johnny Renza had on a white t-shirt and really nice fitting jeans. His butt looked great, a woman notices those things. His eyes wandered the ceiling, deciding whether or not to contribute. Finally, he said, "Guess you know about Halley."

"Halley who?" I asked.

"Leonard Halley. The man who kidnapped the seven-year-old. He sent her father her little fingers, one at a time, until the father told the cops to go fuck themselves, and paid the ransom. Remember? By that time the girl was dead."

"Yeah, I do recall something about that. He's in prison now, isn't he?" I said.

"Sentencing took forever. He's been in the local can all this time. It was Siggy's story, right from the start. It was Siggy who had him picked up. Halley would be naturally be holding a grudge." When Renza said that, Longoria shut his big mouth. "It took the father awhile to get the ransom money together. The police were looking everywhere for Halley, while Siggy was secretly in contact with him. He interviewed him right after the father paid the ransom. Halley had phoned Siggy here at the station, and Siggy knew exactly where to find him. He agreed to hook up with him, with the understanding that he'd come alone and not tip off the police.

"So he had to make a judgment call," Renza said. "Get the interview and run the story of the year... or be a good citizen and tell the cops, in which case he'd have nothing. Turned out Halley admitted that he'd killed the girl right away and kept her fingers on ice, to use later. Even Siggy was shocked. He wasn't sure Halley was telling the truth, but he went ahead and ran the story and *then* told the police everything."

I did remember that. "Actually, I heard they dragged Siggy right off the set, and he caved in so fast he messed himself. They got everything they wanted."

"You'd think that would make Siggy a friend of the police," Renza said, "but they threatened to charge him with conspiracy for withholding information and meeting with a murderer without their knowledge. So everybody was mad. Am I right, Detective Longoria?"

Frank pulled his hat down a quarter of an inch. "He's loose."

"Who's loose?" I asked Filching Frank.

"Halley. He escaped a few days ago, during transfer to the state prison. He's a big guy. He overpowered a five-foot Deputy, took her gun, and is out there somewhere. Apparently, cutting off fingers again."

I couldn't believe I'd heard nothing about this. "Why didn't you share it with the rest of us? For that matter, where's the warning to the public? Don't citizens have the right to know?"

"He's not a danger to the general public." Longoria was adamant. "His crime was premeditated toward a specific kidnapping target. It appears he's done it again."

"Mother of God!" Murray Soper was frozen in the doorway. News directors feel an obligation to be present at the scene of all disasters, not only the ones they create. "What am I hearing? Is this possible? Could an employee of this station have been attacked?"

"The timing fits." Tango Daly's voice was clear and authoritative. They'd forgotten he was there. He'd been wallpaper, listening and watching. "Halley could have relieved Gerald of his finger, and put it in the drawer as a message to the news department. In that case, he'd be retaliating for their reporter's I-D'ing him and betraying him to the authorities." Eyeing the news director, Daly continued, "However, there's a problem with that. Access. How could Halley have gotten in this office to place the finger? Your security specialist must be *really* special, because unless your hallway cameras are the small pinhole type in acoustic ceiling tile, I can't spot them."

Soper started wheezing. He was such a wuss. "There are no cameras. None... anywhere. That would be an invasion of privacy."

Maybe it was the aftermath of My Apartment, or the severed body part, or the general smell in the office, or the phase of the moon, but I completely came unglued. "Invasion of privacy? There's a bloody finger in my bloody desk drawer! How'd it get there? Is anybody in charge here?"

Soper dabbed saliva from the corners of his mouth with his blue plaid handkerchief. "Easy on the whip, Ms. Santini. Try to remember I'm your superior."

"You're an *arse! Ha ha ha ha ha!!!*" That was it, I had officially lost my mind. And probably my job.

But Soper took on Longoria, not me. "When I came here, my predecessor had just been convicted of pushing drugs on these premises; I can tell you there was extreme pressure from the owners to install cameras, and monitor everyone's communication. Legally, employees have no expectation of privacy in that regard, so I could have done it. But I fought it. It *is* an invasion of privacy. I put my job on the line for that one."

Longoria caressed the brim of his hat and carefully moved it back, giving the illusion he was deep in thought. He didn't have much to go on. No intruder caught on videotape. Maybe no prints, since only an idiot would deliver a gory body part without wearing gloves. Still, Longoria was liking the way things were falling into place.

"Well, well, looks like we know who we're looking for. It's Halley," he said. And just like that, the whole thing was over, wrapped up nice and pretty.

It was hard to make eye contact with Soper, now that I realized I'd underestimated him. "That's okay, kid," he said as he stuffed the hanky into his pants pocket. "I'm sending the cleaners in, as soon as the crime scene tape comes down. *Find the rest of him.*"

Daly and I walked out to the car. "Well, that was easy," he said. "Too easy. Something's missing, and it's more than a body. You and I are double-teaming on this one, you're not going it alone. The second they roughed you up, they made it personal."

FOUR

THE TOAD AND I WERE idling in employee parking. Daly had escaped in his luxury mobile office, and I wanted to get away before Longoria came out. Harold Sigmund's two thousand dollar deposit was burning a hole in my pocket. I knew it wasn't a gift, I knew I had to produce Siggy – or the former Siggy. I bet never before in his life had anyone wanted to see him this much. I was giving serious thought to going back to the shoe warehouse for a new pair of patent leather slings, something strappy and open-toed for hot weather, when Soper called. He wanted me back inside. Damn.

I sidled down the hallway past my office and hooked a right into the newsroom. Soper's lair was dead ahead. Squinting through the Venetian blinds, he had a birdseye view of his minions as they busied themselves making mountains out of molehills for the six o'clock news.

This being Saturday, the board on the wall above the Assignment Editor's desk was stuffed with weekend stories, in the absence of Monday to Friday municipal briefings and courthouse follow-ups:

There was a street festival, a Run For The Cure, the regular Saturday Adopt-A-Pet, and an eye cream recall. Apparently when it was exposed to the sun, the cream went to work on your skin like gradient lenses, turning it the color of a chunk of coal for a sort of come-hither raccoon look.

There was a story on some divorced dad with weekend privileges who'd left a lighted doobie wedged into the mouth of a *papier mache'* puppet at his kids' birthday party, and then took everybody out to Klown Burger. Meanwhile, the house burned to the ground.

Fifteen people made it into the Guinness Book of World Records doing something that involved body paint and cauliflower.

But the big news was in Soper's office. He upped my ante. Along with Siggy's salary, he offered to match the month's advance he'd given him if I could find him before the cops did. I asked the same question I'd asked Siggy's brother: "Why me? The cops do it for a living. He could be, you know... dead."

Dead didn't bother Soper. It was the principle of the thing. "I want you to find the twisted sonofabitch. It's a great story."

"Let me reword it: he could be w-a-s-t-e-d. Somebody took off his finger. I can't locate him if he's a corpse, Murray." The list of things I don't like had grown in the past twenty-four hours. Being attacked by maniacs and finding body parts were the latest additions. Dead bodies had always been at the top.

Soper wouldn't take no for an answer. "It could be anybody's finger. I didn't get where I am today by trusting people, especially people like him." I didn't point out he was the one who *employed* 'people like him', or ask exactly where he thought he *was* today. "The little shit didn't have the balls to talk to me in person, or even call. He mailed me a two sentence letter. Tells me nothing."

This was news to me. "What two sentence letter?" I asked him.

"This." He sailed a piece of pale peach Getaway Inn Miami Beach stationery at me. It read: *Gone fishing. Babbo.* It was signed *Sigmund.* "Who the hell is Babbo?" he wanted to know. It was postmarked Monday. Today was Saturday. It had been mailed the day before Siggy bailed. "He didn't even tell me.

God, man, get a grip. You two aren't dating – are you? I told him I'd do my best, pocketed the note and put a hundred feet between us before he could ask anything else. Now I had money coming in from two sources, Harold and Soper, if I could just find Siggy. Renza was just coming out of my office. What's wrong with that picture? "What's up, Johnny?" I asked, trying to sound casual.

"Oh, so now it's Johnny," he said.

"More to the point, what's the sudden attachment to my office, and why are you here on a Saturday?"

"I was driving by and saw the patrol cars."

Yeah, right. He'd have every reason to be in this neighborhood on his day off, in the sexy outfit he used to wear on date night. "What if I said I don't believe you?"

"Just wanted to stick around and hear what Longoria had to say."

"And?"

"And nothing. You look amazing, PJ Want a ride?" That was the line he'd used with great success our senior year. What can I say, I was high on hormones and spring. The ride he gave me was almost a one-way trip to Mommyville. I was one pink strip away from telling Ma to dig out the family christening gown – and hide Pop's rifle – when the Mommyville road washed out. The close call scared the hell out of me.

"I'll pass on that." Back at the car, I didn't dawdle to ponder my future. My head was throbbing, and Ma Santini's comfort food was a mere fifteen minutes away. I felt a sense of obligation to give Harold a call and break the news about his brother's finger, before Longoria did. He went ballistic.

"I knew it, he's been kidnapped! There'll be a ransom note or a phone call. How will they get my number? Maybe they'll call you. Does the station have a budget for this? Because I don't have a lot of money."

"One thing at a time," I told him. "The police are handling this, it's up to them, now." I didn't want to get Harold's hopes up, in light of the early postmark on Soper's mail. Siggy obviously had put some thought into making it look like an abduction, right down to overturning a couple of chairs in the kitchen. He was holed up somewhere with his files, notes, computer and everything, and obviously had no inclination to tell his brother. I didn't say that to Harold.

Tony was waiting on the doorstep when I hugged the curb. He jogged over. "Ma knows!" Most kids' first words are Mama or Papa. In the Santini household, where things are different, one-year-old Tony tugged on my training pants and whimpered, "Ma knows."

"Oh no, what now?" I asked. The butcher job on the finger couldn't have reached home that fast.

"About you in the strip joint on Clinton yesterday. In a real tight *Sweet Enough* t-shirt, gettin' into it with one of the girls, rolling around in the blood and all. Didja win or lose? My money's on you."

It was too late to get back in the car, Ma had spotted me through the curtains. "It was a draw," I said. A little humiliation goes a long way.

The rich aroma of red wine pot roast with bay leaves had permeated the house. Olive oil and rosemary potatoes were browning in the oven. Years of staying out of sight until it was past time to help set the table had honed my senses. I could *smell* that dinner would be ready in exactly eight minutes. Pop was right where I'd left him Thursday, in his chair in front of the TV. He gave me a better-you-than-me look, and went back to flipping channels. Ma was emptying water from the pasta pot.

"You don't look like you've been in a fight to me," she said through the steam. Why are you wearing that scarf around your neck in July? Are you hiding a hickie? Did that girl give you a love bite?"

"No, nothing like that. It's a case I'm working, that's all." I'd stopped wearing the hat because I stopped wearing the bandage. I devised a creative comb-over, to weave my hair over the stitches. It worked, as long as I remembered not to use hair spray... the pain was a religious experience. "How'd you find out?" I asked Ma.

"Blanche DeLuca. She doesn't miss a trick, that Blanche. She got it from Mamie Kielbasa. Her boy Leon said it was such a shame you got roughed up like that. Such a nice boy. A police officer with a legitimate reason to carry a gun." She made a long face and pulled down the lower lid of her eye, as if my reasons weren't legit enough. This is Margie Santini-speak for stop being a private detective and start washing diapers.

"Why aren't you with somebody nice like him on a Saturday night, at home taking care of my grandchildren?" Ma lifted out the meat and scraped the pan for the gravy. I considered grabbing the roast and making a run for it.

Pop made an unscheduled appearance stoveside, in a tissue-thin t-shirt that was about two hundred years old. He palmed his forehead and put his hands on his hips. "Okay, just tell me one thing, and don't get mad. Were you at My Apartment *on* a job, or *for* a job?"

"Pop! How can you say such a thing? Do I look like a stripper to you?"

"Well now, dat's my point. If you need cash, you aren't gonna make much that way. You're not da type. If you need money, you ask me. Okay?"

I didn't know whether to be insulted or flattered. I chose flattered. "Thanks, Pop." I mussed up his wispy grey hair, and he grinned.

Ma wanted to know how he knew what type a stripper should be, and how much money a stripper could make. While he was digging out of that one, Tony helped me cut a good-size slab of meat and pull some potatoes out of the oven. I was right, eight minutes exactly. We put them in Tupperware and lammed it out to the Toad. I could almost hear the engine, over the escalating voices in the kitchen. I told Tony I'd run into his favorite homicide detective today. He said he wished I'd done it with my car.

Sunday morning dawned clear, white hot and bright. I missed it, because I was still in bed. At ten, I showered and threw on black drawstring pants and a white *Made In America With Italian Parts* tank top, and tied on the running shoes I'd bought ten weeks ago for my new cross-training program. They had yet to see pavement.

I'd put off calling Honey for two days now, and I was secretly hoping she wouldn't be at My Apartment on a Sunday. That would mean I'd have to call Daly, fib just a fraction that I'd misplaced Honey's home address, and wait for him to call me back on it. That would buy some time. By then we'd be deep into lunch and, sorry, but I'm not wasting quality eating time looking for a stripper.

I dialed My Apartment. After two-and-a-half beeps, I decided nobody was there. No point letting a phone ring and ring. I'd almost disconnected, when an annoyed voice came on the line. "What."

"What?" I said.

"You tell me.

"Is this My Apartment?"

"Yeah. What." I recognized the slippery, in-your-face Damian. The back of my head pulsed with new pain, and begged me to be smart for once and hang up. Then I remembered Damian had let somebody rip off Sweet Boy. He wasn't going to get away with this.

"Put Honey on the phone," I said in the most kick-ass tone I could muster, feeling tears moving up from my chest.

"Hold on." That was the day I learned it's all in the way you say it. From the sound of her, she was still in another time zone. I wouldn't be driving, if I were her, but I wasn't her. She agreed to meet me in forty-five minutes at New York Grand's, a worn-out greasy spoon conveniently located nowhere near the strip joint, and about halfway to my parents.

Vicky came over as planned, and we left from my place. We could quiz Honey together, hit a few tennis balls in the old Hood and then go eat. The Toad was beginning to grow on me. Whenever I went to get in it, I almost couldn't remember which car it was, it was that unremarkable. Not a bad thing for a private investigator. I killed the engine in the New York Grand's lot. Not to be paranoid, but I had a good look around. No six-foot maniac dressing room divas keeping watch on Honey. No Damian. No other goons ready to finish off the job.

We marched in from the bright sunlight, and the screen door slammed behind us. It took a minute to get used to the forty watt bulbs dangling under the paddle fans. Honey was draped against a wall, leaning back in a kindergarten-size wooden chair. All the tables had chipped black-and-white speckled Formica tops. If she was looking for the one with the highest bacteria count, she'd found it. Honey's real name: Sheila Fuoco. Age: twenty-three. Favorite store: Spandex R Us. Her eyes narrowed at Vicky, and she tossed her hair back, marking her blonde territory. Vicky raised an eyebrow and tossed *her* hair back, in some sort of blonde secret ritualistic attitude challenge.

Honey said she was, umm, sorry about what happened to me at the club. "Elvira... I mean Frances... gets like that when he runs out of money for hormone shots." Nice, but not a legal defense for aggravated assault. Honey said she was putting herself through college dancing at My Apartment. Alas, she'd misplaced her class schedule... as well as the definition of dancing. She'd also misplaced Siggy. Maybe she kissed him with all that lip gloss and he got sucked in. I handed back her key to Siggy's place, and told her I couldn't find the story notes I was looking for.

"I know," she answered. "I've been through it all."

"When? I've had your key."

"Before." Deep sigh, long pause. "Look, I'm gonna level with you woman to woman." I hoped leveling wouldn't require me getting down on all fours. "You're cool, you gave me back my key. I went in when Siggy and Norbert were at work. Only Siggy was already missing, but I didn't know it. I just wanted to see what was inside. It's pretty insulting when your guy throws you over for a *guy*... like you've ruined him for women or something. I wanted to see what they were doing in there." I could understand that. I've wondered, myself. Honey stopped talking for so long, looking right at me, I thought she'd fallen asleep with her eyes open.

"Annnnnd?" I said to jump-start her. I wanted to grip her by the ears and shake her till she went *Tilt*. It wouldn't take that long.

"It all looked, you know, okay. Except the two kitchen chairs were turned over. And, umm, the table was pushed out. There was a piece of paper on it. I kept it. I was mad at him for having such a good time without me."

That was all that Vicky, the queen of female indignation, could take. "You go, girl. Who do these men think they are? Siggy'd better hope you get to him before I do. My ex-husband Mickey, you remember Mickey?" she turned to me for confirmation, completely forgetting I was her maid of honor. "'Anyway, that bottom-dwelling, mouth-breathing freak wrote me one sweet, disgusting love letter after another. Lies, all lies. The whole time, he was joystickin' somebody else. I'm gonna make all the letters into a book. I'll call it *Phallacies*. Clever, huh?"

Honey was befuddled. It was too big for her to process. I shot Vicky a warning look.

"Honey, do you still have that paper, the one you found on Siggy's table?" I asked her. She reached into her Gucci and produced an exact replica of the typed note the news director had shown me. *Gone fishing. Babbo.*

"Who's Babbo, a fishing buddy?" she asked. "I didn't know Siggy liked to fish." She said she had straightened up the chairs and table on the way out of his apartment. And she'd taken the stinking kitchen trash to the dumpster. That's why there was nothing in the pail under the sink when Harold checked it. Honey may have been jilted, but she was a woman with style. Siggy must be an idiot to give her up. What could Norbert ever do for him but hang drapes?

"Okay, Honey. Think back. When were you in Siggy's apartment? I'm not ever going to tell him. This is just woman to woman." Doubt flickered in her baby blues. They were not the innocent eyes that went with her name. They had seen a lot. Maybe too much. *Oh please, don't climb out of your cozy, warm K-hole. Not yet.* "Honey? *When?*"

"I was thinking. Wednesday. 'Cause after that I went for a wax at Star Luxury. You know, every fuzzy little girl down there." She lowered her eyes to the crease in her almost-skirt, and giggled. Star Luxury was a high buck day spa that I could never afford, even if I took that loan from Pop.

Which reminded me. "By the way, just out of curiosity, how much can a dancer earn on a good day?" Pop didn't know everything. Maybe I had a shot at it, in some part of town where nobody knew me. Where the men were drunk enough.

"Oh, plenty. It's all in tens and twenties. They put it in your G-string. Some guys like to tip with their fingers toward you, that way they can cop a feel. Especially if they put it waaaay down low. But then it gets all wet." Toooo much information. I did not need the mental picture of Honey standing in her kitchen, up-ending a soggy G-string and ironing out her gross receipts. I gave her my TV news business card, and asked her to call me right away if she heard from Siggy. The cops hadn't approached her yet, but it was only a matter of time, something I didn't have much of.

"Nice charm bracelet," Vicky told her as we left the table. It had silver micro-penises dangling beside gigantic penises. And little gold condoms. And a pendant that said Home of the Whopper. "You should have it melted down and made into one good .22 round. He deserves it." I grabbed her by the shirt and dragged her out to the street. I probably should have told her more about the case before we went in.

We drove along Hammond and found a gas station with chocolate. "What do you make of it?" I asked Vicky.

"You puttin' me on? After what I just heard, next time I pull out a twenty I'll see it in a whole new light. I'll wash it. Twice."

"*I meant,* do you think she's telling the truth?"

"I think she is. But check this out: I thought I recognized her, and couldn't figure it out, but now I know from where. She volunteers at the no-kill animal shelter. People bring stray dogs and cats into my store, and I take them over to the shelter. Last time I saw her, she was feeding a pitiful looking mama cat who'd just had babies."

"Aw... are we talking about the same Honey?" My opinion of her was improving.

Vicky ran a hand through her hair, snagging all three oversize Mafia princess rings in it. "But then, maybe her no-kill policy doesn't extend to men," she said. "She sure has a motive. A guy throws you over for another guy? Not good."

"But don't you think if a woman wanted payback, she'd take the cutlery to a certain other body part first?"

"You got that right. The jewels. Or their big brother." We both went into the restroom to scrub our hands, just on general principles.

The two of us going back to Lovejoy always makes me feel good. It's our place. It's uncomplicated. You can move away, but you're always a Lovejoy kid. We cut our teeth on its placid stability. "Own up to it, you got a problem with that?" is the eleventh commandment. At a backyard hockey game, if you eat a puck sandwich and get your front teeth knocked down your throat, well, you should have been more careful. Getting in trouble at school was bad, but it was nothing compared to what happened when you got home. Plus, on the walk home, every Italian and Polish mother had already heard about it, and they were lined up outside to give you hell.

When we got bigger, we endured jokes you can only imagine about loose girls in Lovejoy. Certain of us fantasized about living up to that reputation. This meant a lot of quality time – real and imaginary – behind the brick sports equipment building, up against the tennis court at the old park near the tracks.

By the time we left St. Agatha of Catania and headed to public school, every one of us was totally confused about sex. Sex was wrong, unless you had a ring on your finger – I took that to mean through your nose. Short skirts were wrong, too tempting. Snug-fitting panties were wrong, too much rubbing. St. Agatha was the Sicilian virgin martyr, which was how I came to see myself. At the fifteen year reunion, Vicky got hammered and accused Sister Superior of ruining her sex life.

We pulled up to the park. It had become deserted, in favor of newer places to go. The equipment building's two sets of dented steel double doors were still secured with padlocks. Seven feet high and about as wide as a Dunkin Donuts, the bricks were throwing off so much heat, it smelled like a new batch of crullers was coming out. The tennis court had matured into an uneven patch of concrete with crabgrass growing through it.

Everything was pretty much the same, except that the two stay-at-home daddies camped out on the adjacent playground had dumped strollers and cell phones all over the court. They didn't look like they were in the mood to move them. "Sure hope I don't land in that stuff," I said, as we unzipped our racquet covers.

We were chasing balls five minutes, when I faded back to catch a low one and did a header right into the strollers. "Shit!" I moaned, rolling around in the blankies and BlackBerries, "I tripped over my own fucking feet!" A daddie came running. Wow, I thought, now there's a man! As he stood over me with his fists on his hips, I gave him a *You're so big and strong look*, and held up my hand so he could rescue me and show the kids how it's done.

"Thisss is a children's playground," he yelled down, "and that issss highly inappropriate language!"

"*Excuse* me, Bubba?" Vicky got in his face, as she pointed toward the teeter-totter. "See, here's the thing about playgrounds," "That over there, that's for you kiddies. This here, this is paved for players with balls. *You got balls?*"

Daddie was stunned silent.

"*Tsh. Didn't think so.*" Nobody outshouts Balducci. If Vicky and a 767 are revving up in the same hangar, you'll never hear the plane. She inhaled a lungful and giggled, "Sure is good to get in trouble behind the building again. Home sweet home."

We hit a few more balls, but my ankle hurt and my heart wasn't in it. Something about Honey and Siggy wasn't adding up. If Honey was being truthful, she wasn't telling the whole truth. That could be because I hadn't asked the right questions.

When we arrived at the Santini stronghold, Tony barreled toward us before the wheels stopped. He was two leaps away when Ma beamed herself up on the front steps, and unleashed the suffering Italian wail heard around the world. "Ayyyyyy! What now, *a finger*?"

I looked at Tony. He nodded gravely. "I tried to tip you off."

Not inappropriately, The Godfather kicked in on my phone. I checked the text message Inbox:" Call me ASAP. TD."

"Four calls," Daly said when he answered. "Where've you been?"

"On the tennis court in Lovejoy, why?"

"You don't have to go all the way out there to play with balls."

"Yeah, but you won't let me pummel yours on rough pavement and then repeatedly slam them into a brick wall."

"Who knows, could be something new." Never challenge Daly when it comes to the exotic and unusual. Chances are he's been there and done that. I hoped he had not been specifically in *that* particular scenario, as I would want to reserve it for myself, in case he ever deserved it.

He had news from the cops. "Guess what. It was the right middle finger."

"Ouch. Siggy's, right?"

"Don't know yet. Forensics is working it over." I thanked him and flipped the phone closed.

Ma was back at the stove. Pop was asleep in his overstuffed chair. His hand squeezed the remote every time he stirred, and it switched channels. His thumb jerked and called up a cruise commercial. His eyes popped open. "Discovery cruise, my ass. Dere are only three kinds of cruises. Newlywed, overfed and almost dead. You'll never get me on any one of 'em." A man of few, yet profound, words.

From behind, a familiar hand slapped me on the butt. "Yo, Beautiful. How's the red-headed goddess, and her accomplice the blonde bombshell?" It was my favorite cousin from Belleville, New Jersey, Sandro "The Eel" DiLeo, my mother's sister's son. He wasn't my favorite just because he called us a goddess and a bombshell, although that did weigh heavily. He was fun. Plus, The Eel had the shiniest suits in the family. He was connected. He knew stuff. Stuff Ma didn't want to know, because he was her nephew. Stuff Pop already knew, because he was a cop.

Coincidentally, Pop's job had involved a lot of liasing with the feds on mob-related activity. You can imagine the silences at the dinner table, basically from the time Sandro was fifteen and got picked up outside church. He'd wired the confessional for sound, and had been making a pretty good living shaking down the neighborhood's biggest sinners. He considered it helping them to extra penance, and thoughtfully offered a taste to the priest when he discovered the wires sticking out under his seat.

Sandro is one of those guys who seems bigger than his measurements. He's about my height, but with a round face on a square body. Like a cue ball on a domino. His jackets never quite fit. "On account," he explained, "of the muscle training my job requires."

"But you run a pizza parlor," Pop pointed out, soaking up salad dressing with a piece of bread.

"Yeah, exactly. Movin' all that dough." Wink wink. When he laughed, the thin goatee down the center of his chin jumped around. It could possibly have been Magic Markered on.

"I just happened to be in town," he said. Sandro *never* just happened to be in town. My father pretended not to hear. Vicky had begun rhythmically sucking pimentos out of olives from the antipasto plate, causing Sandro to start fiddling with his pinkie ring, losing his train of thought.

We made it halfway through dinner, past the pasta and all the way to the meat, before Tony brought up the finger. "So whose finger is it?" he said.

I choked and reached for the wine. "Thanks for waiting until after the rigatoni swimming in red sauce. How'd you find out about it, anyway?"

Ma jumped in, lest Tony take credit for her extensive communications network. "You think these things are a secret? That smartass detective Frank Longoria told his mommy; and she told Antje Pooler. Antje has her hair done – not very well, I might add – Saturdays at three at Connie's Clip Joint. "

"Is that it? Where's this going?" I asked my mother as I turned the empty glass over and shook it.

"Connie told me this morning, at poker practice after Mass. She's a lousy hairdresser, but a great poker player."

"You have poker practice?" I still couldn't believe my mother was playing.

"You bet your *braciole*. Got to keep your hand in, for the Executive Game."

"Aw, geez," Pop burbled through a mouthful of meatballs.

Tony persisted. "Back to the subject, which finger was it?" He was rounding up the extra tomato sauce on his plate. I couldn't look.

"Right middle." That shut everybody up. Except Sandro.

"Oh. Middle? Oh. That ain't good. Oh. A finger's one thing. Middle finger, that's somethin' else."

"How would you know?" Pop smirked. Everybody got real quiet. The knives were squeaking on the plates like fingernails on a blackboard. It made the fillings in my teeth hurt. But I thought since the subject was already out there, I could brief Sandro on the situation, give him the Headline News version, and maybe he could shed some light.

"I'm gonna go out on a limb," my cousin said, "and articulate what everybody's thinkin'. It's a message. If it's your friend Siggy's middle finger in your drawer, it's a message to *you* – which I myself would take very personally on your behalf, but that's for later. If it's somebody else's middle finger, it's a message to *Siggy*." He helped himself to more meat and slashed into it, making wet, squishy noises. "Let us assume it was Siggy who was supposed to find it. It's the middle finger. He's pissed somebody off, serious-like. It's a statement. He's outta time, his clock runneth over. And the TV station better back off whatever he was workin' on, *capice*?" I got chills. Siggy must have been hot on the heels of exposing organized crime, and he got too close. Why couldn't I get a good story like that?

Then Pop surprised everybody. "Thanks for clearin' that up, Sandro. I mean it. I didn't want to have to say it. It's the mob."

Then Ma surprised everybody. "That reminds me. Nonna Giovanna will be here next week."

"Nice segue, Ma," I said, reaching for the gallon of Gallo and pouring it to the brim. "For a visit?"

"Forever."

Nonna Giovanna, the Sicilian who watered our lawn with gasoline, was bringing all her stuff and moving in. Swooping into my old bedroom upstairs, beside Tony. "What will she do here all day, away from the herd in Palermo?" I asked.

"The herd's dying off," Ma said. "She'll do what she does every time, watch Home Shopping Network, 24/7. The only good English she knows is from the Florentine gold salespeople. God help us if she ever gets a credit card." Ma bit her knuckle. "*Marrone*, she can't, can she?"

The evening wound down and died a natural death. Pretty much everything had been said by the time we polished off the cannoli. I had to stop eating like this. Sandro gave me his cell number, and I promised to call and talk some more before he left town.

Downtown Buffalo was Sunday-night-quiet. There wasn't even a breeze off the lake. Only the occasional siren in the distance, some emergency I was glad I wasn't part of. It was nine by the time Vicky and I got back to my building and drove around to visitors parking. "You've been strangely quiet all night," I told her. "What are you thinking about?"

"That cousin of yours. He sizzles."

"Excuse me? Not that again You say that every time. Sandro is adorable, but trust me. You do not want to go there."

"Has he ever been married? I'm like a moth to a flame with that guy. Did you see the way he flirted with me over the marinated red peppers?" She got out of the Toad and opened the door to her red Jeep. It had *Balducci's Love your Dog* printed on the side, with a daffy looking Golden retriever panting all over the *Love.*

"Don't do it, Vicky. That flame burns red hot. I can already smell your hair singeing "

"*Guastafesta.*"

"I am not either a party pooper!"

"Janice, he's been coming to see your parents for years. Coincidentally, so have I. He's family. I'm almost family. It's better than a dating service. It's the perfect way to meet a man, totally legitimate."

"Except *the man* isn't," I felt compelled to point out.

"Give me his number, Santini, or I'll tell him it was you that requisitioned the .45 he lost in the couch cushions ten Christmases ago."

"Still no. You can't prove that. And anyway, finders keepers, Santini family rules. You do that, and I'll have no choice but to tell him about how you stole his Calvin Klein briefs from the guest room and kept them under your pillow for half a year."

"Honey, I'd do that today, if I could get 'em fresh off his fabulous body. But okay, then at least do this: ask him more questions before he leaves. Like who he knows and why he's here. I'll help you!" She peeled out of the lot onto Lakefront. I bit my lip as the Jeep's taillights faded into the lowering dark, hoping I wasn't pulling her into something that really was too hot to handle.

I scoped out the lot, looking for who knows what, and went in through the garage, shivering as the grate came down behind me. At the elevator door, the ElectroPass on my key ring flashed red as usual, and did an electronic handshake with the security unit. Access to elevators and stairwells is by ElectroPass only. Visitors have to go to the main entrance and get by the concierge between 8 a.m. and 11 p.m. After that, a resident has to physically go down and let them in.

I live in the middle building of a trio of ten-story towers overlooking Lake Erie, imaginatively called Erie Towers. Four good-size apartments to a floor. Wide-angle cameras above the twin elevators capture each hallway, with more lenses located in the three levels of underground parking. I hate being watched like that, and out of habit flipped a one-finger-salute as I went by. The concierges at the monitoring desk didn't care. They'd been military police and had seen worse than me. Tonight, I didn't mind the cameras so much. In fact, I hoped the new guy, a civilian, would be as vigilant.

Relaxed and alone in a long, summery cream colored cotton shift, I considered how I was pouring wine like water, yet it didn't seem to be having much effect. So I poured another teeny glass of red and snagged the phone... then hesitated, walking the length of the balcony. Seven times. That would qualify as pacing. Through the sliding glass doors, my bedroom looked lonely. So did the living room. And the dining room.

I could call Johnny Renza just to talk, but then he'd want to come over. Then I'd say yes when I meant no, and no when I meant yes. I peered into the darkness and asked Buffalo Light what I should do. The lighthouse flashed green for call, and white for are you nuts? In my head I could hear Etta James singing *you better love it or leave it alone.* So I dialed Daly instead. He answered on the second ring. "Hello, beautiful."

"Okay, I have my number blocked. How do you always know it's me?"

"That's my job. What's up?" He had me on the speaker phone.

I kicked back in a lounge chair. "I ran the Siggy thing by Sandro. Pop got in on it. Never thought I'd see them agree on anything, but they both think the mob's involved." I told Daly what Sandro had said about the middle finger being a message to Siggy.

"Maybe. That would make it not Siggy's finger. Can you line up a meeting with Sandro before he goes back to the Pits?" I didn't know where Daly was from – nobody did – but when you're in Buffalo, everybody calls New Jersey the Pits. "While I find your cousin's taste in clothing lacking, he would have a unique perspective on uses for detached middle fingers, horses heads being so passe.'"

"What's wrong with Sandro's clothes, too much polyester?"

"Too much Glock." Daly hates status symbols, especially when it comes to the hardware. He's such a Sig-Sauer snob. A Sig semi-automatic is expensive but basic and dependable, but not flashy. To men who carry as part of their work, gun ownership is a competitive sport, although they can't agree on how it's graded. It's because of the testosterone. That doesn't account for my own total comfort with a Sig, but that's another story. I think it has something to do with a woman's being in control of something smooth and solid that will go off whenever she's ready, with no strings attached.

The wine was gone already. I stared at it in disbelief. "I'm calling Harold in the morning," I told Daly. "Maybe he's got more to say, with the finger and all. By the way, why am I on a speaker phone? What're you doing while we're talking?" I asked at my own risk. Pause. Exhale.

"Oiling my gun."

FIVE

I'D BEEN SOUND ASLEEP. In my dream, I was on a game show with an empty shopping cart. I had two minutes to fill it with as many pairs of heels as I could. I was just planning my strategy down the evening sandals aisle, when my cell phone rang. I squeezed my eyes closed and flipped open the phone.

"You know who this is?" the voice asked me at 7:30 a.m.

"What am I, psychic? Who the hell is this, and how'd you get my number?"

"Harold Sigmund. Sorry to call so early. The police want me to identify the finger that was found in my brother's... uh... your desk. I was wondering if you'd go to the Medical Examiner's with me."

Now? Was he nuts? "Harold, honey, they can't start without you. See you there at ten." By the time I hung up, the game show was over. The leopard three inchers with ankle strap and delicate gold buckle had floated away in a big soapy dream bubble. Damn.

I put on coffee and showered. What's the appropriate gear to wear to the viewing of a finger? I started with the shoes, beige pumps with a thin four-inch gold heel. Plain tan slacks, and a lime top. With my frizzy red hair, I looked like a snow cone on fire. Two cups of coffee and a fistful of almond kisses later, I was reaching for the front doorknob when the house phone rang.

"Give me his number," Vicky said. No hello, no how are you, just give me his number.

"Hell no." I hung up. While I waited for the elevator, I listened for the house line to ring again. It didn't, which meant Vicky would advance to Plan B. I dreaded whatever that was.

The finger would be in a forensics lab, where tests were performed on anything that used to have a social security number. This lab was a one-story, rundown flat-top building on Clinton, not far from downtown, in fact right down the street from My Apartment. Convenient, in case Frances missed any more estrogen shots and some other visitor came up a few body parts short. I slid into the gravel lot ten minutes late. Harold wasn't there. I left the car in an unnumbered space in front of the unnumbered building, and went inside.

Frank Longoria was cooling his heels in the vestibule. The only thing that had changed about him over the years, other than his rise to fake legitimacy, was the addition of a squiggly little mustache. He still had the same greasy dark hair, cut with garden clippers. Same cocky angle to his head. Same cloying roach spray aftershave. I was killing time by the glass doors so he wouldn't do something stupid like talk to me, when Harold walked in.

We followed Longoria down a frigid, pistachio-colored shower stall of a hallway lit with dull florescent bulbs. It reminded me of my office. He gave a push to door number three, and we were inside a laboratory with microscopes and specimens on slides. Also specimens not on slides, which made my stomach recoil. I recognized the formaldehyde smell from senior year biology, when we kept the cats we were dissecting in a barrel with our names on tags tied around their ankles. If I had to do that today, I flat out wouldn't. Another plain clothes detective was waiting, next to a guy in a lab coat over a Buffalo Bills t-shirt and jeans.

"Forgot to ask you to check your gun at the door," Frank chuckled at me, "but with your aim, I don't think that's a problem. Anyway, it's already pretty damn dead in here." Dead. Asshole. I gave him a "Lucky for you there are witnesses" look.

Harold was bouncing off the walls. "Could we get on with this?" he said to Longoria, who nodded to Buffalo Bill, who brought out the jar. A pale finger with a gold ring floated in clear liquid. Harold's hand went up so fast, he almost broke his nose. "Not good, this is not good!" The garlic he was burbling up smelled like it had been fermenting since New Year's.

Frank sniggered and leaned back on his heels, listening to Harold hurling outside the door. I angled over the counter to take another look at the ring.

"Know what it means?" I asked.

"Yeah. Confirms he's a guy, a real ssssweet guy." Frank's teeth were dazzling. He must have just had the blood cleaned off.

I took in the long tables with lights chained over them, and panic set in. Everybody looked hostile. They all had big, painted funhouse eyes. What if I never left this room? What if they kept me here in jars, who'd ever know?

I kicked open the door and moved toward daylight, down the long, echo-y hallway, slipping on Harold's barf. Chunks of something that looked like scallops were creeping down the wall onto the linoleum.

I found Harold by his car, buffing up with baby wipes. "I use them to clean my hands before I work on hard drives," he said, mopping his face. He scrubbed every bit of exposed skin, and offered me a wipe.

Longoria was on our heels. "So? Yes or no?" he pumped Harold.

Harold struggled with the answer. "Yes. It's my brother's. Who would do such a thing? I never thought it would come to this. Is he... dead?"

"Not necessarily." Frank twirled the keys to his midnight blue unmarked Ford Crown Vic on his finger. "I have to level with you, it looks like Halley's work. He's showing the TV station that nobody gets away with using him and turning him in."

"But that was a journalistic decision," I said to Frank, jumping to Siggy's defense. "Nobody knows what really happened. Anyway, you seemed to like it when he did it."

"He should have called us when he first heard from Halley, not after he went into business for himself." Frank held up his hand when I tried to answer. "Water under the bridge, too late now, we'll find him. Halley's here somewhere. He's our man." Longoria spun out of the lot.

I shook gravel out of my hair and turned to Harold, who was assessing dust damage to his Mercedes. More baby wipes, then a clean handkerchief. Ugh. So Longoria thought this was Halley's work. I thought about Sandro and Pa's other theory that the mob could be saying Siggy had gone too far. But with what?

"Did Siggy take something too far, Harold? Because this isn't adding up. Halley is not a messenger boy. He's not creative. He's a demented, violent, nasty person who kills little girls and chops them up. He doesn't get into the nuances of hidden meanings."

"I can't imagine what you're talking about. I can only tell you what I know. It's my brother's finger, and I've known him all my life. Can I go now?" Point taken. It was Siggy's ring, too. I asked him one more time who his brother's friends were. Nada. He said Siggy led a dull life. I reminded him Siggy was shacked up with a guy who wore fancier teddies than me. At which point Harold abruptly cut the chitchat, and trucked his Saks two-piece back to the computer store.

The way I saw it, the suspect list had just quadrupled: Halley, and that still seemed too easy. Honey, the bubble dancing animal lover who Siggy threw over for a guy. Norbert Dojka, Siggy's new main squeeze, who maybe didn't like the way Siggy made hospital corners on the 400-count Hartwig's sheets, and Harold, Siggy's own loving blood relative who obviously didn't give a rat's ass whether Siggy lived or died. I called Hartwig's department store and asked for Dojka. He hadn't been to work for a week. Family emergency. I looked at my watch. 11:04 a.m.

On the off-chance Tony could spring loose, I called his cell. "What's the cutest brother in Western New York doing today, and when are you taking lunch?"

"Just Western New York? I'm in Cheektowaga, on Charlotte. Putting digital boxes in a house that smells like cat pooh. Lunch when I'm finished, if I can still eat. Why?"

Perfect. Harold lived in Cheektowaga. "I have a proposition for you." I filled him in on Harold's identification of the stray finger. "Your buddy Longoria isn't even considering Harold as a suspect, he keeps saying it's Halley. Frank sure would look stupid if Siggy's brother turned out to be the killer. Wouldn't that be nice? I need to get into his apartment. You, cable guy, could get the key from the super."

"But isn't Harold paying you to work for him?"

"Only a detail," I said. "You want to skewer Frank or not?"

"I'm there. But I can't take more than an hour for lunch, know what I mean?" Sweet Tony was a poster child for forgetfulness. He was on probation at work. He almost got canned after he wired thirty homes in a new subdivision with cable outlets – including complimentary potty and closet access that was not in the contract – and then forgot to hook everything up to the main line. Nobody knew it until the houses sold. Blocks of high bucks HDTV's were on the snow channel.

I took Jefferson up to The Kensington and cut across to Cheektowaga. Harold's neighborhood was new. He lived on a street of cookie cutter apartment buildings, really out of character for such a particular guy. Each two-story rectangle was wrapped in beige siding. Access was plentiful, entrances front and back, and iron stairways at each end. Good news for Tony and me, but it could also be Grand Central inside, with residents coming from all directions. Parking was to the rear. It didn't add up that Harold would leave his Mercedes in such a high traffic area.

Tony hopped out of the van. "Looks like barracks. The architect musta been in the Army. This is gonna be fun." He slung a webbed work belt over the part of his shirt that had *Tony* embroidered on it, and went next door to find the super. I slid down to my eyebrows in the front seat. The builders had bulldozed all the vegetation, so there weren't any good bushes to lurk in. He came back beaming. "First floor. Let's go."

We stood outside Harold's door and listened. Nothing from inside. Music down the hall. But Harold only three minutes away by car. I held my breath... and turned the key. It took a minute to realize the door wasn't opening, because Harold had installed his own deadbolt. Maybe he wasn't such an idiot. "Here, hold this," I shoved my shoulder bag at Tony and rooted around for my lock pick. It had come out of its case, and was tangled in my hairbrush. "Nudge me if somebody comes."

Tony hummed the Zamboni song. "This is illegal, isn't it?"

"Only if we get caught."

"I'm hungry."

"I have to pee." I couldn't get the tension right. The tool kept slipping, and I was sweating. It was so hot, it had to be a buck-eighty in the hallway. I was scrunched down and bent over. Everything hurt. "We're in!"

It looked like a techno nerd's dorm room. Everything was lined up, real sterile. There were no coffee table books on how to cut off fingers. Just to be sure, I checked the knife drawer. Nothing in there screamed "I just carved up his brother!" We had twenty minutes before Tony had to leave; less, if I spotted Harold's Mercedes pulling in through the open blinds. I didn't know what I was looking for, but nothing looked wrong... no ladies' underwear, no crack, no meth, not even a joint. Also there were no pictures, and no personal items. *He doesn't live here*. You'd never know he'd even stepped inside the door... unless you explored the beautiful, old fashioned lawyer's desk. Now, *this* was Harold Sigmund. Polished walnut, with a huge moss green leather writing area decorated with gold filigree around the edges. A quality product.

Sitting on top was a cognac-colored padded leather address book. Inside the front cover, where it said "Property Of", he had carefully printed "Harold Sigmund," as if he were expecting Alzheimer's to set in any minute, and he wouldn't remember. Most entries were initials or nicknames with phone numbers. I copied a few.

"Good clean fun?" Tony wanted to know.

"No way to tell, yet. No names."

The laptop was more interesting. When I pressed the Enter key, the monitor came to life and a spreadsheet popped up. Rows of numbers danced as we watched. They changed constantly, going on a run, stopping, running again. I opened an internet browser and played with the explorer bar. Favorites included all seven days of the week. Every one went to a page that required an access code. Another link went to the television station system. This would enable him to use his computer as if he were sitting in the newsroom. Or in Siggy's office. Siggy might have done some work from here.

I closed the browser and tried the drawers. They were crammed with printouts of *AN-AmeriNews* wire copy, straight off the computer. Even more than Siggy had in his office. All with the same slug as Siggy's: *Costa Rican drug bust*. I lifted a few from the center of each pile and stashed them in my purse. There were newspaper clippings about busts of small drug boats filled with cocaine that had been off-loaded from big ships. The stories said fishermen made a good living taking fuel to the boats. One hell of a story. Maybe I could finish what Siggy had started.

"Okay, Tony," I whispered by the door. "Step back before we go. What looks like it's been moved?" I knew Harold would come home and find the deadbolt open. Maybe he'd think he'd forgotten to lock it. Maybe he wouldn't ask the super if anybody had been around. But he'd still suspect. He just wouldn't dream it was us.

I took one last look over my shoulder as Tony tugged the door behind us, wondering what we'd really found out. "No, wait!" I jammed my arm between the door and the frame, and howled as the wood carved a dent in my wrist. There my keys were, catching the light on Harold's grey carpet. Tony slid in and snagged them. We yanked the door shut and scurried down the hall in opposite directions, then turned and collided on the way back, tee-heeing like six-year-olds.

As our two vehicles peeled out of the lot, Tony leaned out and hooted, "This is one thing Ma *doesn't know!*"

Home never looked so good. Half an hour on the treadmill and another half of rowing and weights took the jitters out of me. I showered and slipped into the cloud-soft fuzzy socks and pink yoga outfit I'd bought just before I didn't sign up for classes. The pink had the look and texture of Hostess Sno-Balls...and I heard the real thing calling my name from the freezer. So I got them out, caressing the coconut through the cellophane. I saw on television how you can diet by collecting all the sweets in the house and freezing them, the theory being you can't eat them frozen. Wrong. I called Wei-To-Go and ordered the General Tso's Lunch Special with free pot stickers; and I holed up in the condo for the rest of the day.

Padding into the dining room, I piled the computer printouts from Siggy's desk onto the table. Next, my overstuffed purse turned loose the printouts from Harold's apartment. What was I going to do with a mountain of copies of exactly the same story? They were years old, but still crossing the wire. The damndest thing I'd ever seen.

29 Jun 2007 10:00EST C. Rodriguez

SAN JOSE (AN) – The Costa Rican government has announced it has arrested 9 people, and has confiscated nearly half a ton of cocaine, in its latest sweep of international drug shipments from Colombia. The cocaine originated in Colombia, destined to pass through Costa Rica either by land or sea.

In a separate incident, the U.S. Coast Guard intercepted another boat and drove it to shore. It was turned over to Costa Rican authorities. That boat was empty and is believed to have been laden with drugs that were off-loaded at sea, not long before. Three Colombians are being held. Costa Rican authorities say the boat was capable of carrying two tons of cocaine.

It was equipped with four 200-horsepower outboard motors and carried 30.5M gallons of wire fuel.

Wire service stories always have a distinct time and date stamp near the slug – along with the name of the writer. That way, news operations can glance at a whole truckload of stories with the same slug and see which one is the newest version. I lined up Harold's printouts on the left, and Siggy's on the right. Comparing according to time and date, letter for letter and number for number, the two brothers' versions matched... except that the copy changed in the subtlest way.

This was getting me excited. I veered into the kitchen and dug into the silverware drawer for a pen. On a paper towel, I made a list of what was different about the stories: dates, times, writers' names. In the last line, the gallons of fuel varied. Also, some versions ended with "cash fuel" and others said "wire fuel."

Just for the hell of it, I pulled out the long roll of paper from Siggy's machine. If it came right down to it, as far as I was concerned this would be the official version, directly from *AmeriNews*. Days and days worth of news was still on the roll, in the exact order in which *AmeriNews* had sent it. This meant nothing could have been removed, and the Costa Rica story should be identical to the computer printouts. I went to the day and time on one of Siggy's printouts, and compared it to the machine. The printout version wasn't even there. I tried another date, another time. Same thing. Over and over, until the paper ran out and my eyeballs crossed. *AmeriNews* was not sending out this dull old story, yet somewhere between there and Siggy's computer, it was pushing itself back in.

Who would care about a two-year-old dead story? Why would it be updated? Why would both Siggy and Harold collect them like seashells? And how could they not show up on the machine?

I stuffed a Sno-Ball into my mouth, and twenty bucks into the palm of the Wei-To-Go delivery boy. Sugary chocolate and Chinese, taken together, are known to improve the thought process. Just to be sure, I opened some mystery wine. Sometimes it's the label on a bottle of wine that seduces me. I soak it off, then have no idea what's inside. This one surfaced last Christmas when Ma drove over, tied on an apron, and rooted around in my cupboard to personally repossess her big iron skillet, the skillet that she said I was insulting through lack of use.

"*Ahm ashempt*," she proclaimed, invoking Nonna's broken English for "I'm ashamed." This was purely for effect, since my mother was born in Brooklyn, but not without a sense of drama.

"Why is it necessary to wear an apron just to pick up a frying pan?" I'd asked her.

"It's no frying pan, it's a skillet, and this is proper *cucina* attire. Show some respect for the kitchen. I bet you don't even own an apron."

"You're right, Ma, I don't. I can screw up Minute Rice, remember? Clothing is not an issue in my kitchen. You can be buck naked if you want."

"Aha, what's *this*?" she said, pulling my good black lace panties out from the bottom shelf. All this time, I thought the maid had taken them.

"Hey, you cook your way, I'll cook mine. Say, is my red corset in there by any chance?"

"Think about your future, Pommie. What would Officer Leon Kielbasa think if he saw something like *this* in your kitchen?"

"Ma, trust me, he'll never get that lucky."

I left the Costa Rica write-ups sitting on the table, and settled onto the couch with General Tso and the remote control, to catch the last of the afternoon news. They were just wrapping it up with one of Renza's pre-taped fluff pieces on the weather. I envisioned him standing in my office that first day, telling me Gerald Sigmund could be AWOL or DOA... *or in Costa Rica*. He'd backed off when I asked about it. I thought he was clamming up because he really didn't know, but maybe there was more. He came back on camera. "John Renza,reporting."

My eyes narrowed until I was squinting at the television like Larry David. *Renza, you know something.* Time for a sit-down. I had no idea what I was going to say, so I dialed before I lost my nerve, and let it ring. We'd covered a lot of territory together, and it didn't happen without some good ole Santini creativity.

When I was seven and he was eight and we played house, I got him to let me be the one who was gone all day with the briefcase. He did the dishes and he swept the porch, and his payoff came at bedtime. We pretended we were wrestling, and he got to be on top. There were a lot of symbolic body slams south of the border. Afterward, just like our parents, we pretended to be satisfied and go to sleep.

Eight rings. He took his time. It made me think about how he'd taken his time at my Sweet Sixteen. Ma was inside serving punch, and Johnny was out behind the house in the October snow seducing her daughter. All night he'd been whipping me into a frenzy, teasing me with smoldering looks. He was older, wiser and faster, with a body that was teenage solid and rock hard. He eased past my fluffy pink angora birthday sweater, and went to work on my bra. Little did he know, all he had to do was ask.

The thing that stopped me was Kathy Shula, the original good time that was had by all. Saturday nights, she was busier than a mustard paddle in a kosher deli. Rumor had it Renza was the one who'd primed her pump – hers and half the girls in the eleventh grade. It was too late to turn back time, but now that I was older and maybe wiser, I sure didn't want to be on his Greatest Hits List.

Renza picked up. "What took you so long?" I asked. To hell with hello. Now that I thought about it, he didn't deserve it.

"Just taking care of business." He sounded preoccupied.

"What, do Shula and her love monkeys make house calls?"

"You're never going to forget that, are you? That was high school."

The way I saw it, high school was only a warm-up. "I couldn't care less," I lied.

"You always were a lousy liar. Just remember, way before high school I was the only boy who let you wear the pants."

"Which you've tried to take off ever since."

"On at least one occasion, it was not my idea. As I recall, you were trembling."

I was trembling just thinking about it. I slapped myself hard, and it passed. "You're rotten to the core for bringing that up. I called because Siggy still hasn't surfaced, and I think there's something you're not telling me. Do you know what story he was working on?"

He hesitated. "He... never told me."

"That's not the same as saying you don't know." The slimebag was avoiding the question. "*Do* you know?"

"The answer is no. The guy was always typing and phoning, phoning and typing, all hush-hush, but nothing ever came out of it. I can't believe he still got paid. Now apologize for accusing me of lying."

"Okay, I apologize, I blamed you unfairly." Holding a grudge was no good. It wasn't his fault Kathy was a slut. Yes it was. "So what are *you* working on?"

"Now, that I really can't tell you. Although it would appear you and I are talking to some of the same people."

"Who?" My little heart was galloping in eager anticipation of a breakthrough on the Costa Rica mystery. I could let bygones be bygones long enough to collaborate on a great story, find Siggy and collect the rewards. "Tell me who!"

"I really can't say," he answered flatly. I asked him how he knew it was the same people, and he wouldn't tell me that, either. The pocket rat had done it again, lulled me into the warm fuzzies, then sucker punched me right in the gut. When was I ever going to learn?

"Fine. Next time you need something from me, don't ask."

"I think you'll be asking me, first. By the way, just so it's no surprise, Kathy Shula was in talking to Soper today. She's back looking for a job.
"

"Why, are you doing a special on prostitution?" I hung up before I could say more of what I was thinking.

This whole scenario was totally unacceptable. I didn't believe Longoria's theory about Halley, not for a minute. Daly was right, it was too pat. The only way I was going to find Siggy and turn this into cold, hard cash was to solve the puzzle of what he was working on. So I stuffed a fistful of wirecopy printouts into my purse, along with the last Sno-Ball, and made for the station.

After the evening news, the place is always deserted. Only two cars were left in the lot. They belonged to the lone reporter and photographer, who were out to dinner somewhere in a news truck, sitting in a fast food parking lot with double fries, triple cheeseburgers and a cell phone, listening to the police scanner and praying nothing would happen while they were gone. Next signs of life would begin around 9:30 p.m., before the eleven o'clock show. So I had about two-and-a-half hours to myself.

I went through the newsroom computer by computer, and tried every single one. I tried calling up the Costa Rica story in every way imaginable, especially on Renza's terminal, where I was dying to spend extra time, but didn't think it was such a good idea. There could be hidden cameras in the newsroom, whether Soper knew it or not. It wouldn't be the first time. As it was, I had the feeling I wasn't alone. My heart was thumping in my chest. At that moment, I understood completely I had stumbled across something critical and hazardous to my health, and I almost crumbled under the weight of it: *The story simply does not exist outside of my office. Somebody is going to die for that, and I fuckin' hope it's not me.*

I scampered over to my office. The yellow police tape across the door was down. The lights were on, sparing me forty-five minutes in the dark waiting for the fluorescents. The place had been cleaned, just as Soper promised. I couldn't identify a single remaining smell as Janice barf. Or Siggy finger. The computer was sitting on a brand new desk.

I gave thanks to the angels who protect inquisitive idiots like me, and dropped down in front of the keyboard. This time I knew exactly where I needed to go: I tapped in *Wires.Priority.Local.Weekly*, then *Costa Rican drug bust*, and waited for the computer to find it. There it was, the exact same one I'd printed out.

Just to be sure, I checked it against Harold's and Siggy's printouts. Bingo. This story showed up only on two computers, this one and the one in Harold's apartment. But it had not come up again since Siggy disappeared. Both he and the story were gone.

Something in the stillness of the empty station caught my attention. The police radios across the hall had fallen silent, as if they were listening, too. My ears rotated like a German Shepherd's. I peered across the hall into the reporters' area, hoping the evening crew had come back, but they hadn't. At the far end of the newsroom, I imagined the top of a head scooting out of sight. If somebody popped up and went *Boo!* I'd vaporize.

I tiptoed down to the ladies' room and eased inside. Backing up against the door so it wouldn't close, I scrunched down to see if there were feet in the stalls. Even fear has a sense of humor: *What if I look and there are three?* Nothing. The room was empty. *Be careful, someone could be standing on a seat.*

"Stop it," I whispered to myself. But what about the men's room? Forget it. I wouldn't go in there in broad daylight, and I certainly wasn't going in there now. What if our photog had returned and stopped in for a pee? I'd gotten a lot of questionable PR in the last few days, and I didn't need to add men's room grazing to the resume'. So I went back to work, feeling vulnerable.

Then the other half of the sound came... the outside door closed. *I wasn't alone.* Someone had come – or gone. Weapons are not legal newsroom gear, but from the time I was old enough to understand, Pop taught me a policeman's saying: It's better to be tried by twelve than carried by six. Save yourself, then let them charge you if they want. So I slowly sprung the Sig loose from the Velcro, and waited. It was so quiet you could hear a subpoena drop.

A person wouldn't have to be Iroquois to slip down a carpeted hallway without making noise. I moved over to the door, sucked in oxygen and steadied myself against the silent *AmeriNews* machine. I leaned out by degrees, gun ready, praying somebody else wasn't doing the same thing on the other side of the wall. It took forever. Just as I got one eye exposed, the machine woke up with a thundering clang and threw me off. Its typewriter keys lumbered across the paper, rhythmically shifting spaces and spitting out copy. It scared the living hell out of me.

"*Mother of Pearl!*" I shrieked and fired off a round into the ceiling. After that I was half deaf from the ringing in my ears. I slung my purse over my shoulder, wrapped both hands around the Sig and took off down the hall. The sickly yellow lights that hung over the parking lot illuminated a third car that hadn't there before. A dull white sedan, a Ford. If some poor employee had just gone inside and gotten the fright of his life, I'd feel really stupid.

My butt slapped the seat of the Toad and I hit the door lock. No sooner did I throw the shift into Drive, than blinding headlights from the Ford lit up my windshield. My foot slammed the gas pedal. The car stalled out. *No! Not now!* Toads, mere loaners, are ugly but *dependable* – they're not supposed to stall! I took a huge breath and tried the key again, and the car fairly jumped off the pavement. We burned rubber out of the lot, took the Sherbrook corner on two wheels, cut across Bishop and ran the light on Chapel. The Ford was right behind. I tried losing it, throwing in right angles. The car stayed with me on the first one, then I thought I'd lost it. But it was idling when I got back on Sherbrook.

Either I was the biggest rank amateur, or the tail already knew where I was going. When I finally pulled onto Lakefront and whipped a fast left into my parking garage, the Ford stopped and lingered on the street. Words can not express how happy I was to see the security grate sealing the moron out.

From the garage there was no way to watch that car, or see who was in it. Same thing from my windows, which took up a whole half floor on the water side of the building, and unfortunately not overlooking the street. Normally that was soothing, with the water all dark and mysterious. Tonight it was ominous. Buffalo Light was flashing in a low mist, warning me to get off the balcony and go inside, so I did.

But I couldn't resist hanging out the window, craning my neck to see the street. I couldn't tell a damn thing, except that somebody the next building over was looking back through binoculars. I flipped him off. "Pervert!" Stupid, too... even I know you don't use field glasses so close to a window when there's a full moon.

SIX

GEORGE CLOONEY WAS a shoe salesman, and he was kneeling at my feet. I was running my hands back and forth across his short-cropped hair. His gorgeous brown eyes met mine meaningfully, as he pulled a fire engine red pair of Stuart Weitzman patent leather four-inch stilettos out of the box. He cradled the arch of my foot in his hand, rubbing the underside meaningfully, and began to slip the shoe over my toes. Then the pounding began. "Son of a bitch – go away!" I hollered behind my sleep mask. "No, not you George, keep going. George... George?" He had left. The pounding started again, louder. "Geez, *what already*?" Now I was really mad. I'd been up half the night, and it had taken the other half to fall asleep. I wasn't out of bed yet, and already I'd been deprived of sleep, shoes and the prospect of mind-blowing dream sex.

I stalked to the front door and yelled through it. "It's eight in the morning. *What*?" Through the peephole, I focused on a tan, rested and ready Johnny Renza. He was wearing his linen blazer over denims. That was really hitting below the belt. How could he do this? How could I resist? Plus, he was holding up a big bag of carry-out from Arnaud's. Arnaud's makes the best hot New Orleans beignets. They sprinkle them with powdered sugar. I could smell the coffee.

"Breakfast delivery." He said with a crooked grin.

"How'd you get past Javier?" I asked back, as I spit on my fingers in the mirror and used my nails to scrape mascara from under my eyes.

"Why don't you let me in, and we can talk about it." I had every reason *not* to let him in. I looked like a post office Most Wanted photo, I felt worse, and I was allergic to men who had no problem seducing me and then dumping me for a pair of big bazookas... whose IQ, by the way, isn't as high as her tire pressure. "Open up," he said. So I did.

"Good thing I got here when I did," he said as he popped the tops off the steaming coffee and unloaded the beignets onto plates. "Still hot."

"The beignets or the coffee?"

"You, sweet thing. Still lookin' good in the morning." I ignored that. The coffee was kicking in. He had me at a disadvantage, because I was already half undressed. My favorite sleep gear is no gear. All I had on was the *Property of Buffalo Athletic Dept* shirt from the laundry pile.

"So what brings you here, and how *did* you get past Javier? Tell me, so I can fix it." Javier Calderon was the new concierge-slash-security guard. The condominium association had stopped springing for the salaries of former military policemen who took no shit from anybody. They held auditions for anyone who could speak English, fit into a 42-Long navy blazer with an Erie Towers crest on the pocket and didn't drink out of a paper bag. Before this job, Javier worked at the ketchup plant out on Luskie.

"Told him I was your older brother," Renza said. "Told him it was a surprise. He was very polite." He took off his jacket and slung it on the back of a dining room chair.

"I didn't say you could stay," I said halfheartedly, wolfing down a beignet. "That extra coffee for me?"

"Yep. You're back at the station, but we never see each other, unless you're coughing up body parts. You call, but we play word games. I don't actually get to set eyes on you. Are you avoiding me?" Renza tore off a piece of beignet and held it to my lips. My mouth opened automatically. It's important not to let your glucose drop below Mayday level. We played at that awhile, then I woke up and realized what was going on. He had just sucked powdered sugar off my fingers, and was tracing the inside of my lower lip with his pinkie. My canines put some notches in it, just above the nail.

"Shit, Janice! What now?" He rocketed into the kitchen to wash off the blood, but there wasn't any, big baby. He covered the distance back in a second, and pulled me out of the chair. If I had red marks on my arms, it'd be his fault. And I wouldn't wash them for a week. "Whatever you're thinking, that was then. This is now." He kissed me hard, like they do in the movies, pushing my head all the way back. Like Gable and what's-her-name in *Gone with the Wind*.

My pulse was twitching down where Little Janice used to do playtime with little Johnny on top. He eased off and ran his palms across my back and down my butt, while his lips moved on mine in slow, light circles. Johnny felt rigid against me. His tongue ever so softly slipped into my mouth, and I began to suck. My knees went weak. What would be the harm of a Tuesday morning quickie?

"Sure, I dated other girls when you were married," he said without losing contact. "What was I supposed to do?" You notice I didn't get married."

"That's because your fiancée caught you kanoodling with the maid of honor in the choir loft during your own wedding rehearsal," I murmured softly, not wanting to blow my one shot at a good orgasm over something so trivial as foul organ play.

"She told me she wanted to show me a surprise for the bride," he said.

"And?"

"It wasn't for the bride."

"So what really stopped you?" I asked.

"The marriage wasn't right. She wasn't for me. You were," he whispered into my mouth. At another time, on another planet, I might have bought that. "I still care about you," he said. "Let me show you how much." He reached under my top and squeezed my nipples, which were already on high beam. I yelped. He knew exactly how to hotwire me. We'd never make it to the bedroom. We didn't even make it to the couch. Or the floor. I unzipped his pants and ripped the shirt off his irresistibly smooth Mediterranean olive chest, as he lifted me onto the table. He leaned over and I could smell his skin. An old familiar intoxication swept over me.

He jerked my shirt off over my head in one swift movement and reached for a beignet, tapping it to shake off loose powder. He dusted my breasts like snow...then my belly...then greedy Little Janice, who was hungry and starving for more. We never lost eye contact as his tongue lapped at my nipples. Then he concentrated on making little wet circles on every inch of exposed skin between my mouth and my knees. I'd had no idea he was so talented, and was jealous of the bitches who had taught him. When I didn't think I could stand any more, his tongue and his fingers came back up and began multitasking until everything was drenched and sweet. I came so loud the windows shook. I didn't care about anything else when he pulled me roughly against him and filled me with his stiffness and his heat, over and over and over. When I came again, I was bound for glory.

Afterward, dazed and satisfied, I buffed up in the bathroom and tried like hell to wipe the stupid smile off my face. I wouldn't waste time assessing what all this meant. Primarily because by now Renza's testosterone would be back under the legal limit, and he'd be back to thinking about his next oil change. Little Janice was still twitching, and I told the slut to stop. For now.

"So, what are you working on these days?" he said as I waltzed into the living room in my bathrobe and sank luxuriously onto the couch cushions next to him.

"You wouldn't tell me what *you're* working on, so why should I tell you?"

"We might be able to help each other out," he said. I doubted it. Renza was a great reporter. One of the reasons was that he kept his ears open and his mouth shut. Except for a few minutes ago. But I'm nothing if not a gambler, so I dangled a morsel of information in hopes of picking up something. The man knew everybody.

"I'm not sure, but I think Siggy might have been working on a big drug story and somebody got wind of it and clipped him," I said.

Renza liked it. "It's possible. But then, there's our friend Halley, and the whole finger thing. Halley has a motive, too. Siggy did turn him in. In a psycho sort of way, he has a legitimate beef. And isn't Siggy living with a man? What about him? You know how they get when they're mad about something. Maybe Siggy wore mismatched underwear, satin when it should've been lace."

I started to say I knew for a fact it was Norbert Dojka – not Siggy – who wore the fancy stuff, then caught myself. I'd lied to get the key from Honey, and breaking and entering is a bitch to explain. So I changed the subject. "I think Siggy has a brother," I said. "Blood may be thicker than water, but who knows. What do you think?"

No answer. So I plowed ahead. "C'mon, Renza. You know something, I can feel it. What about his old girlfriend. How do you kick out one lover and just truck in a replacement?"

"You kidding, Janice? Happens every day. But even if Siggy made a fool of her, she wouldn't necessarily want him dead."

"Yes, she would." I had Kathy Shula written all over my face, and he shut up.

Then he started asking the questions. "Siggy liked to swing both ways. Did you find any girls' numbers in his desk?"

"Why, you want the leftovers?"

"Dammit, Santini, you asked me what I think! Maybe girls were drug contacts. That's a dangerous business. What about phone numbers? Addresses? Houses, apartments, motels?"

I gave in, and went and got the Stickies and the piece of cardboard and showed them to him. He looked bored. He put everything in his pocket and said he'd give it some thought, like it was a big imposition, and get back to me. "Okay, sweet thing, it's a work day, gotta go. Hope you liked breakfast." He put his hand on the back of my neck, which he knows drives me wild, and bent down for a kiss.

Lightning bolt. At that exact moment, I knew that Cupid had torpedoed me. "Holy shit! Did you wear a condom? Did you?" Panic. I grabbed him by the shirt collar, and came forehead-to-forehead. "*Did you? Where is it?*"

"Oops. It sorta took both of us by surprise, didn't it? It'll be okay, Janice, really. God smiles down on women who fuck before 8:30 Eastern."

"Get out, get out! Is this a new game? Feed Janice and watch her get stupid? Go!" Renza blew me a kiss and pulled the door behind him.

"Oh holy Christ!" I howled, pounding my head on the wall. "Not again, no, not again! People this gullible aren't meant to reproduce! Stupid, stupid, stupid! I can't go through that again!" I could hear the train to Mommyville whistling down the track. This time it might stop.

I did a half hour shower blitz, all the scrubbing up a girl can do under the circumstances. I marked the date on my calendar, as the door knocking started again. Renza was a dead man. I rushed the door armed with my hot hair dryer and threw it open.

Tango Daly was angled against the elevator wall, very casual. He was in black, head to toe. Today he had a big chrome Tag-Heuer strapped on his wrist. Sunglasses loose in his hand. Short sleeve silk. European-cut drapey slacks that would be soft to the touch, if you ever wanted to touch a man again. His mouth was smiling, but his eyes weren't. He made a living appearing to be something he wasn't. Only people who knew him well could tell the difference, and I could tell he wasn't happy. He took in the heavy breathing and the dryer. "Experts say there are easier ways to blow a guy."

"Where'd you come from? Was Javier at the desk?" I sank deeper into my robe. "Why do I even ask."

"Told him I was your brother. He said it must be family reunion day. He winked at me, Janice. That might not be a good sign for you." Daly moved past me to occupy the foyer. He took a look around. The dining room was a wreck. Baked goods, coffee, sugar everywhere. It looked like Aunt Jemima had shagged the Energizer bunny. "There's been sex here."

"Cooking accident," I said, pulling my robe up higher.

"Bullshit." He walked the perimeter of the table, a jungle cat, slow and sure. "Looks like your other brother was planting seeds of discontent. Or something else." He helped himself to some bottled water out of the fridge. I felt kind of woozy, and wondered if it was too soon for morning sickness. I wiped down the table and got rid of the evidence, then went into the bedroom to throw on jeans and a tank top, while he waited on the balcony. I came out primed to change the subject.

Daly was primed to hit something. "Where'd you get those red marks?" he asked, nodding toward my arms where Renza had plucked me out of the chair. They'd turn passionate purple by noon. I rolled my eyes and fished in my purse for Siggy's wire copy to show him, then realized it was still sitting on my desk at the station. And the door to my office was wide open. Well hell, there hadn't been a lot of time for extras, last night. TV news is a scary business, but I'd bet money I was the first reporter at *that* place to end the workday by shooting her way out to the car. At present I was a satisfied woman who would need an inflatable donut for the next week. I wished the world well, and didn't really care if Gerald Sigmund was dead or if the mothership had come to get him. *Try, Janice. When the condo fee comes due, you'll care.*

I filled Daly in on the whole Costa Rica thing, and showed him an example of copy off the *AmeriNews* wire machine, compared to printouts from Siggy's computer that actually showed the mystery story, along with similar printouts from Harold's drawer.

"Hold it," he said. "Harold gave you these?"

"Not exactly."

"Well then... you didn't."

"I did."

"Access?"

"Tony got the key from the super."

"Santini," he said with a sly smile, "you are one wicked woman."

"I learned from the best." Something about Daly made me want to put my head on his shoulder. Any other day, I'd choose another destination. "By the way, this might or might not mean something," I said. "Harold's a computer freak, so this could be perfectly natural, but his laptop had links to lots of sites that read like days of the week. They needed password authentication, which I didn't have. And there was a spreadsheet with numbers jumping around like fleas on a coonhound."

He whipped his BlackBerry off the belt clip and punched some keys. "Daly. When was the last time you ran a story on Costa Rica drug trafficking?" he asked whoever answered. "Alpha Oscar? Roger that." The man had contacts everywhere. A breeze had kicked up off the water, and clouds were rolling in from the north.. He squinted behind his aviators while he thought things through.

"Alpha Oscar a relative?" I asked.

"AO: Area of Operations. *AmeriNews* hasn't written a story like that in over half a year. The United States has been cruising the Costa Rican coast, heavy into picking up cocaine offloaded from large ships onto boats bound for Mexico. The area of operations is wide. Concentration is based more on water than land. Roads through Panama are too rough to make Central American land running any fun. That would actually be a solid news story," he mused, as I planned what to wear when I accepted the Peabody Award. "But something about it stinks. If *AmeriNews* didn't send it, then the write-ups on Gerald's and Harold's computers are bogus, like you said. Maybe Gerald was a journalist playing with the facts, or maybe something else. Who knows, about Harold."

Daly squinted into the water. "Siggy was either developing some big story he stumbled across, or *he is* the story. My guess is that either he uncovered a drug operation, or was part of one."

I had to laugh. "Get out, Siggy a contraband mover? The journalist voted most likely to jerk off to stay awake at the Edward R. Murrow Awards? On the other hand, Ren... er, another reporter... also thinks he might have been involved with drugs."

"It can happen. Watch the quiet ones, Janice. Me, for instance." Daly fixed his eyes on me. There were a lot of questions in them, questions about what had just happened on my dining room table. I looked away, but it was too late. He already knew.

"So where do we go from here?" I asked as we moved inside. He could take it any way he wanted. "You sure you still want to help me find Siggy? You've got lots of better things to do."

He gripped my wrist by the table. Twice in one day, again...when it rains it pours. "Amateur," he said evenly, eyeing the powdered sugar on the floor. "Rank amateur." Then he brushed the red on my arms ever so lightly. It about lifted me off the ground, and I started shallow, high-altitude breathing.

"I want to make this clear," he intoned evenly. "This is separate from your dating game. Someone hurt you. Whoever it turns out to be, I will not cut slack." Then Daly kissed the tip of my nose and moved toward the door. On the way, he flipped a folded paper onto the table. "The car your other 'brother' absconded in today."

I snapped it up. "But Renza drives a red Camaro," I said stupidly.

"Apparently not for everything."

Under a "Dick's Sport and Guns" logo, Daly had doodled two hearts and scrawled: 1999 Ford Taurus SE, white.

Damn it, how long had Renza been following me, and why? Fortunately, I'd notched some good size scratches into his back, just to cover my options. Explain *those* to Kathy.

The sky was thick with charcoal clouds, and the stifling air clung to me like a wetsuit. The forecast called for afternoon storms, and it was already two o' clock. If it rained maybe the heat could escape, god knows the humans couldn't. Nobody was in a good mood, and this probably wasn't the best time to nose around the cops. They have zero use for private eyes. Journalists come in second on their shit list. Since I was both, you can guess how happy they'd be to see me. But I was willing to swallow my pride and beg. At this point, they were the ones with access to everything about Gerald Sigmund.

I thought a good place to start would be Leon Kielbasa, the nice officer whose socks my mother thought I should be at home washing. He worked out of Homicide, and turned up every place Longoria did. Unlike Frank, he had human genes. But he was pulling the evening shift and had gone out on patrol early.

How could it be, that in all the noise of the shift change – footsteps, phones, duty gear coming and going, conversation, radios – my ears would pick up the single voice that could wreck my entire afternoon? "You're under arrest," it said.

"I didn't think you came out during the day," I countered. It was the good Detective Longoria, what a surprise. "So what are the charges?"

"Depends on your answer. Come with me." I followed him down the hall to Homicide. Detectives at two of the desks stopped what they were doing to watch. I knew one of them. Harper Frasier, cute as bug in a rug.

"Hey, Harper, how's it hangin'?"

"Gettin' no complaints." He winked at me and gestured toward Longoria. "Maybe you want to drop breadcrumbs." He propped his ankle on his knee and rocked back. We had high school history. Should have had more. A couple of movies, a couple of moves. Football team. He always loved making Frank crazy. I was with him, on that.

Longoria shut the door and slithered behind his desk. "Okay, what do you have?" he asked point-blank.

"I was going to ask you the same thing."

"Here's how it works, Janice. We're sure we know where Halley is. That's not my job, he'll be picked up. I want to know what *you've* got. I know who you've been talking to, and when you've been doing it. If you have anything that could be considered evidence in this case and you don't turn it over, I'm going to slam you for obstructing justice."

I thought about that. What could I have that he'd want? He wasn't getting my copy of Honey's key, he didn't need it, anyway. He could go inside Gerald's place anytime he wanted. Anything out of Harold's apartment, he could kiss my lily white Sicilian butt for, he'd never get it.

If I even said I'd been there, I'd be admitting to B&E. As for the stuff from my newsroom office, the Stickies with the names and the numbers, Renza had them and they were not technically in my possession. Mental note: get them back. That left the wirecopy and Siggy's printouts. Those were from my own office, but okay, I could throw him that bone.

"The only thing I can imagine you'd be interested in is something that's mine in the first place. But I'll give it to you and even throw in my take on it, if you promise to keep me posted on Siggy. Fair?"

"Turn it over, and you might not get charged. I'll see what I can do about the rest." I knew he wouldn't. Asshole.

So I forked over the printouts I'd shown Daly that morning, and pointed out the discrepancies. He looked them up and down quickly, like he was checking for spelling mistakes. If he hit on the drug conclusion same as Daly, he never let on. Finally, he looked up. "This has zero to do with Halley. It's nothing. And that's all you have?"

"That's all I have, I swear," I said.

"Anything new you get, I want to see it right away, understand?" It was terrifying to think of the power this man possessed. I stared at him for a long moment, and he dismissed me with a wave of his claw. So I ditched Longoria at his desk... hunched over the printouts, wings folded, picking for fresh meat.

Harper Frasier grinned as I coasted by. "Your fingers were crossed," he said, "I saw them behind your back." I'd forgotten, *he* was the man who paid attention.

It was like Ghostbusters. Something evil was seeping through every crevice of that building, and it was called Longoria. I rolled the Toad around the corner into a taxi stand, to think things through. If Longoria knew that Halley killed Siggy, and he knew where Halley was, why was he leaning on *me* for something extra? If he thought it wasn't Halley, then it could only be that he wanted to find out how much I knew.

But why me? If I were Frank, I'd be looking at insurance policies and family feuds. Harold had expensive tastes. Every part of his brother, except for the right middle finger, had been missing an entire week already, and Harold's only big concern was spiffing up his Mercedes. Speaking of Harold, Frosty the Snowman started playing on my cell, the ringtone I'd assigned to him because the man was so cold he peed sleet.

"Did you get Siggy's papers so I can pay his bills?" he started.

"Not yet. You saw for yourself there wasn't anything in his apartment, and I didn't find them in his office. Just squiggles about various Miss New Yorks."

"I'd like to have those. They're my brother's personal possessions."

And all this time, I thought Harold wasn't wired for sentimentality. "Sorry, Harold, I threw them out. Didn't realize they were that important." Silence.

"By the way, somebody's been into my computer," he said.

"How do you know?" I asked. *He's fishing.*

"Somebody's been into my computer," he repeated.

"You already said that, Harold. How do you know?"

"Computers are what I do. Some snot-nosed amateur has been snooping around. Why would that be?" he asked.

"Search me. Did they do it online, or at your place?"

"See, that's the thing. Certain web pages were pulled up – they're on passwords and the login wasn't initiated. But how would anybody know what sites to go to, if they hadn't been in my apartment on my computer, where I've got them all bookmarked?"

"Like I said, Harold, this is the first I've heard about it. I don't know anything. Who do you think it is?"

"Somebody who drops her keys."

Holy shit, holy shit, *Ho-ly-Shit*. He had the friggin' place under video surveillance!

"You ignorant bitch. For a private investigator, you don't know very much. It takes ten minutes to rig cameras. For me, five."

"But..."

"What are you, stupid?"

"I... was just..." I stammered.

"Back off, PJ You won't see me again. But I'll know where *you* are, every minute. Oh looky at that, the nice officer's writing you a ticket, you stupid, dimwitted, red-headed bitch."

"Excuse me? Stupid, dimwitted *redheaded* bitch? Never insult the hair! *You're* the stupid one, you geeky bullshit artist with no crops on top and no life!"

A uniform knuckled the window and I rolled it down. "You a taxi?" he asked me."

"Do I freakin' look like one?" Maybe not the best answer, but the only one that came out.

"Special delivery," he said. I took the ticket. My head did a staccato bang against the steering wheel. How... fucking... embarrassing.

I screwed my head around but couldn't see Harold's Mercedes. He'd played me like a violin. First, he got me to get Honey's key and let him into Siggy's apartment; then he made sure I didn't have the information he wanted in my office at the station; then he got me on videotape, nailing me on breaking and entering into his apartment, so he could hold that over my head. And now I had him on my tail, too. Everybody in Buffalo was tracking me. Renza... Harold... Daly...the cops, it was a damn procession.

By the time I arrived back home, I was wrung out. When Daly called, I had just undressed. So as not to belabor the point, I gave him the Headline News version: Longoria's still a maggot, Harold's gone to ground, Tony and I snagged starring roles in a B&E. Film at eleven.

Daly chuckled. "Next time wear a bag over your head. Meet me in forty-five minutes at Rocco's. It's important. And don't wear any of that pink yogi crap."

"Yoga crap."

"That either."

"But..." He hung up.

"Lesson time," Daly started, when I dragged into Rocco's Gym. Only one mirror, and I'd stay clear of it. I knew the mirror thing was irrational, but my head still hurt. "You need to know how to take care of yourself."

"I already know," I told him. "Black belt, remember?"

"Obviously," he said as he fished around in my hair to see how the stitches were coming. "I'm going to show you close-up defense moves that could save your life. How to wipe out a guy in the front seat of your car, or in a phone booth."

"I don't let guys in my car, and I have a cell phone." Ordinarily I'm not opposed to learning, but Harold had sucked the will right out of me. Plus, did Daly ever not look hot? He was barefoot, in loose black pants with a drawstring waist, over a black t-shirt that fit like a condom over his spectacular chest. I mean glove... it fit like a glove. It wasn't a very big room, but it was wall-to-wall with equipment. "What's that thing?" I asked about a gadget you sit on with your legs straight in front of you on pads. It didn't look like it did anything at all.

"It's a leg stretcher. You use it to get a good split, so you can make high side kicks. Get on, I'll show you." I lifted a leg onto each long brace. Daly squatted and twisted a thingamajig in the middle, and my legs separated like two slow trains at a fork in the track. "Tell me when to stop." They went wider, wider, wider. "Now? How about now?" I'd be damned if I was going to let him think I was a sissy. He stopped anyway, and stepped back to have a look at PJ making like a wishbone. He crossed his arms and looked thoughtful. "I like it. It's you." He was doing it again, dissolving my clothes with his eyes. Little Janice shuddered a time or two, and I made him help me up. We angled between weight stations onto a workout mat, and he made me take off my shoes.

"Always remember this: Your gun has its use, but your body is the only weapon someone can't take away from you and use against you. Meet Chuck. He likes to be kicked and punched."

Chuck was a flesh-colored, soft plastic torso of adjustable height, on a water-filled base. Truth be told, he reminded me of Daly. Strong jaw, muscular, he looked capable. Daly showed me how to execute an elbow strike. Rotate the waist away from your opponent, make a fist and raise your bent arm so the elbow lines up with his face or throat or anything you can connect with. Now rotate back like the wind. "Let 'er rip." After five or six tries, I was hammering Chuck pretty good.

We worked through a few other moves. My favorite was the one where I pretended to knee Daly in the groin, and when his head went down I grabbed it like a football and plowed my knee up through his face. "Okay, stop," he said. "You like this one too much. Last one for today: head butt." Be still, my foolish heart. That is one cool move. "Instead of running away, never be afraid to grab your opponent by the shoulders so he – or she – can't leave."

"Excuse me? I can't hear you, because I'm hauling ass in the other direction." Maybe this stuff wasn't for me. I was no hero. In fact, I was shocked I didn't piddle my pants in My Apartment.

"He's already in your face. Deal with it. Dig your nails into his shoulders, turn your head away forty-five degrees, and pull him toward you. At the same time, ram the edge of your forehead into the center of his." I liked the sound of that, but it didn't go too well. I tried it on Chuck and almost put myself into a coma, and Chuck was only soft plastic.

All in all it was a productive three hours, and I drove home with new confidence to contemplate where my investigation was going. I fell asleep in the fetal position on the couch, sucking salt out of potato chips and Merlot through a straw from a glass on the floor, watching Sex and the City for the five hundredth time. Carrie was head over heels, and Mr. Big was still in it for the fun. It was a horror movie.

When I came to, around noon, I threw on some pink yogi crap and went for a fast walk. When I limped back, the message light was blinking. Three hang-ups, number four was Harold's syrupy voice. "Sorry we missed your call? That's lame, you can do better than that. Redheads shouldn't wear pink. The green you almost put on looks better. Be very careful today."

I played it four times, and every time my acid indigestion started burning higher up. My whole throat was burning. Harold was spying on me, and it had to be through a window. I eyeballed the front door. It was locked. I made sure the windows and sliding glass doors were locked, too. I pulled the drapes, even on the water side, and checked the last call. It was from Ma. She had a surprise for me. Plus, Sandro had brought struffoli for dessert, and I should come to dinner. If you can call it dinner, before evening rush hour.

I had to give Sandro credit, he never arrived empty-handed. I have a weakness for *strouffoli*, cranberry-sized fried balls of dough mixed with slivered almonds, stuck together with honey, sprinkles and tiny pieces of citron. Only the unimaginative eat them with a knife and fork. They're gooey and fabulous and finger lickin' good.

For a change, my arrival at the house went off without a hitch, in fact the yard was deserted. Something was weird, different. The air was still and the birds were quiet. And then I saw it by the front door. The

Sicilian three-legged stone plaque with Medusa's head full of snakes in the middle. *Maddone*, it was back on the wall. This could mean only one thing: Nonna Giovanna was in the auditorium.

"*Cara! Cara!* You're on the money, on the money!" Nonna chanted from the kitchen, through a pink fog of tomato sauce and garlic. Pop looked heavenward and went back to flipping channels.

"Lawn's greening up, Pop," I told him as I planted a smooch on his head.

"Ya got only two options: let it get brown or water da hell out of it." He kept the chitchat short, so as not to say anything that might throw a wrench in the meal prep. I dropped my purse on a chair and shuffled into the kitchen to break off a fistful of bread to dunk in the pot.

Nonna brandished her stirring spoon and lunged at me. An outsider might run from this, but I knew it was only the precursor to the Black Embrace. Nonna was Sicilian from the top of her four-foot-eleven-and-a-half-inch frame to the soles of her size fives. She still had only one basic outfit, with occasional variations, and it was all in black. The naturally curly Brillo pad she wore for hair was three inches long all the way around, no exceptions. At Halloween, when kids stopped screaming they wanted to know where she got the wig. People thought she didn't speak English until she opened her mouth, and then they were positive. She got practice only during visits to Lovejoy, when she stockpiled new phrases from television. Along with Home Shopping Network, she'd joined Ma in soaking up *Sopranos* culture.

"What happened?" I asked Nonna. "Pop said last Sunday you were going coming, but today's only Wednesday." My family usually doesn't move that fast.

"Extraordinary, Pommie! Time is of the essence! Any fuckin' fool who puts the *maloik* on you is gonna take the long walk, *capice*?" The *malocchio* – the evil eye – is nothing compared to the wrath of Giovanna.

"Your mother told her about da strip joint," Pop singsonged from the easy chair. "She was gonna find out anyway."

"Thanks, Nonna," I said, "but no more burnings on the front lawn, okay? I'm going to work this whole thing out myself."

"Your cousin Sandro's a good boy, you should listen to him. He says somebody's been leanin' on you," she waved the spoon in an arc. "An' giving you the finger!" On 'finger' she thrust the spoon skyward, like the Statue of Liberty. A big glob of tomato flew off and glued itself to the drop ceiling.

"Her room's right next to mine," Tony said with a wink, leaning over the back burner to get a contact high from onion vapors. He's in love with Nonna's red sauce, and calls her the Italian Scallion. Needless to say, Ma is not impressed. It's heresy to question your owe mother's tomato technique. I gave his T-shirt a two-thumbs-up. It said *Leave the Gun. Bring the Cannolis.*

"C'mon," he motioned, "I wanna show you somethin'." I followed him upstairs to his room.

"What, are you still hiding rabbits under the bed?"

"Not since Greta chewed through the TV cable." One of the neighbor kids got a cute little rabbit named Greta on a recent Easter, and Tony wound up adopting her. "I did have her litter trained. And it was no big thing replacin' the phone cord, and the USB. But when she tore up the coax, well, that's goin' too far. It took a lot for me to give her up."

Yeah, I knew. Before Greta, Tony had Spring Roll, a Vietnamese pot-bellied pig that rooted up the wall-to-wall carpet all the way to the top of the stairs. The old rug needed to go anyway, but the snorting was too much for Ma. Even through ear plugs, the pig and Pa kept her up all night.

"Here, look at this." He pulled a king size three-ring notebook off a shelf and proudly handed it to me.

I flipped through two hundred pages of empty lined paper. "So?"

"It's for Nonna's recipes. I'm gonna secretly ask her for one every day, after Ma goes to bed. Then I'm gonna use 'em to open a restaurant – lunch only at first, a few tables, nothin' fancy. Got some cash put away. Carmine an' me got it all worked out."

"Carmine can eat, that we know, but can he cook?" He's Tony's best friend, a three hundred pound Insinkerator who hasn't missed a meal since... ever.

"You got no idea. We've been practicin' over at his house. We got our eye on a little place near Elmwood. We'll call it *The Garlic Cove.* Paint the inside with grottos and sea stuff and fishin' boats. Cove, not Clove, get it?"

"Not only do I get it, I'm very proud of you."

"Plus, my beautiful sister, this is somethin' else Ma doesn't know!"

When we got back to the kitchen, Sandro appeared in the doorway and the room officially became too crowded to turn around in. He had outdone himself. Grey poly suit with a luster you could line your lips in, and a nice Armani break where the pants met the spectator pumps. Black shirt, white tie, enough Brylcreem to grease an eighteen-wheeler.

"What, did Vicky get a better offer," he said, flicking imaginary lint off his shoulder. He always ended sentences down, even questions.

"Was she supposed to be here?" I asked my hopeful, horny cousin. He and Vicky together... it would be reciprocal insanity. "She asked about you too, and...ow!" Ma squeezed past to the sink, pinching my arm and twisting really hard. This is the Santini warning shot over the bow, the signal to clam up or else. Over the years, my body has been a billboard of bruises, from one end to the other. Sandro draped an arm across my shoulder and hustled me out to the far end of the dining room.

"Been doin' some askin' around, know what I mean. Checkin' the locals, the Gambruzo family. 'Course, I have not made the acquaintance of these individuals personally. But they got more connections at your friendly downtown cop shop than Reddy Kilowatt, if you get my drift. And accidents can happen. Evidence can vaporize. People, too, I might add."

"You got names?" I'd never asked him for help before, because I didn't want to owe. But things were changing.

"It's comin'. Allow me to intercede on your behalf."

"Caaaareful," Pop chimed in from the living room.

Sandro lowered his voice and put his pointing finger on my sternum. "Not for nothin', but when is an investigation *not an investigation?* When a cop is *not a cop*. Think about it. Word to the wise, watch your step, that's all I'm sayin'. Your name will not be mentioned."

"Thanks," I told him gratefully, although I wasn't exactly sure what he'd just said.

"No problem. I am especially talented when it comes to dealing with queeries."

"You mean queries."

"Yeah, whatever."

SEVEN

"SO WHAT'LL WE DO ABOUT the *mezzofinook*?" Nonna Giovanna said about Siggy, talking through a mouthful of dessert *strouffoli.*

"*We* aren't going to do anything at all, Nonna, although I sure would like to know where he is. And how do you know he's a *mezzofinook*?" I asked.

"From what you said. AC/DC's nothing new. We got 'em in Palermo, too. In fact, this week they're on special, and aren't they exotic." Livia Soprano meets the *Florentine Jewelry Hour.*

My purse started barking *How Much Is That Doggie in the Window*, Vicky's ringtone. First words out of her mouth: "I want Sandro's number."

"No."

"Yes, Santini."

"No, Balducci."

"Oh. Is that Vicky." Sandro bellowed behind me. "Where is she."

"I heard that, that's what I thought. Shame on you!" Vicky said. "You know how psychic I am. I'm there in five." I sighed, snapped the phone closed and got ready to go. She was probably just around the corner. Pop would have to tweak the air conditioning to deal with the blistering heat between Sandro and Vicky. She'd be sucking the honey off his *strouffoli* before he could say Yo. Besides, I had things to do. I still needed to talk to Leon Kielbasa and find out what Longoria was doing with the Costa Rica story printouts he'd pilfered from me.

"Pommie! Don't go away, don't touch that dial!" Nonna trailed across the grass. "Protection's my middle name!" she breathed as she dipped and swayed, waving red ribbons and whipping a string of garlic like a propellor, intoning mysterious Sicilian phrases.

I got winged by a clove, and dived into the car. The Toad blasted off just as Vicky planted her Jeep on the front walk. Nonna lurched out of the way and stood watching me solemnly, wringing her hands as I turned the corner punching in Kielbasa's number.

"Hey, Leon, how's life?" I said when he answered.

"Not bad. Heard you were in to see Longoria yesterday."

"Something like that. Actually, I came to see you, and he hijacked me in the lobby. I wanted to ask how the hunt for Sigmund, or his killer, is coming along."

"Okay, that's not really our thing anymore. Not much of a mystery. Longoria's pretty convinced Halley clipped him out of revenge. We just need to locate Halley. We've got good intel that he's holed up with his old girlfriend, Yeulah Hilroy. Why they didn't even try to leave town, I don't know."

"Halley is the only suspect?"

"Yep. We've moved on to the Tobin murder-suicide."

"Wait a minute, Leon, hold on. You're on the Sigmund case with Longoria, right? Frank didn't even mention anything to you about what I brought in yesterday, all those computer printouts of a news story? All the discrepancies in the numbers and the words? I mean, they're just little things, but he really squeezed me for them. Nobody's checking them out?"

"Nope. I got no idea what you're talking about," he said.

"But it's a good lead!"

"It's a *dead* lead. Not my call. Sorry, PJ, I'm not the big guy, and I don't run the show. I don't enjoy the nine course meal, I just shovel the shit afterward." I thanked Leon and hung up. Maybe my mother was right. Leon was pragmatic and uncomplicated. He'd never have a nervous breakdown over an incomplete murder investigation. If he could live like that and go home to a nice, peaceful evening with his wife and kids, maybe I should be there waiting for him, washing the diapers.

Or, you could just shoot me now. The rest of the way home, I ran through the list of likely suspects in what was looking more and more like a death than a kidnapping. Who still had a motive?

Fact: Siggy had an interest in drug smuggling. And since the same Costa Rica computer copy turned up at Harold's house too, Harold could be involved.

Fact: Siggy had dumped Honey for Norbert. Maybe Honey wanted revenge. Vicky had a point. If a guy did that to me, I'd want to try out that groin-knee thingie. Speaking of Norbert, where was he? I made a note to check with Hartwig's department store again.

Fact: Siggy had angered child killer Leonard Halley, by telling the police where he was. Even if the cops did practically smack it out of him, maybe Halley wanted payback.

Fact: Siggy owed money to personal trainer George Cabral, never mind why. Maybe George was coming after him for payment. But if George got carried away and killed him, that'd also kill his chances of ever getting his money back. I kept him on the list, just in case. First thing in the morning, right after I talked myself out of working out, I'd drop in on Cabral at Jock's Gym.

---

8 a.m. I think. I was only up because I'd pulled something on that damn leg stretcher at the gym and still couldn't find a good sleeping position. I brushed my teeth and then couldn't remember whether I'd done it, and had to go back to see if the brush was wet.

Coffee, showering and shaving my most important real estate took thirty-four minutes. All this was only a run-up to the most important part: an hour of makeup, dressing and chocolate-filled buttery croissants. A woman needs her nutrition. Then I motored over to see George. I took The Kensington to Linkage and turned north on Pryor.

Jock's Gym was open for business, and already you could smell the humid sweat from the street. I wanted to go in, but those damn mirrors, I could not take them. This place wasn't anywhere near My Apartment, but it wasn't the highest class gym in town, either. It'd be just my luck that Frances would use this one to bulk up. I wouldn't recognize him without his Elvira wig and glittery gold lashes.

There's the fightin' side of me, and the chicken side of me. The chicken side said to wait in the car and tail Cabral when he went to lunch, and I told the chicken side that sounded like a plan. Even if he skittered out through the back wall, he'd have to hit the street via the exit right in front of me.

I dug around in the glove compartment for food, and came up with a melted caramel and a packet of candy corn, two fast food ketchups and a wrapped peppermint. Disgusting restaurant freebies are absolutely golden in an emergency. I was halfway through the candy corn when George came screaming out of the lot and skidded around the corner in a dark blue Porsche Boxter with the top down. He was probably sitting on encyclopedias to see over the steering wheel. I've got a theory about guys and Porsches. It's probably the same one you've got. But then, if I were such a genius psychoanalyst, I wouldn't be sitting in a no-name rental car, staking out a fireplug who's driving a very expensive sports car, just so I could buy groceries.

I pulled out onto Pryor and kept a good distance, just barely making the lights behind him. We headed west, and I mentally ticked off all the places he wasn't going – basically anywhere that had anything to do with me, thank god. But the territory was getting real familiar, and when we got to Hertel I knew why. We took a right at the Fill 'n' Go, and rolled up to 1361 Leonardo. I eased up against the curb across the street, and watched George pull into the lot. He shoehorned the Boxter into a slot next to the side entrance of Gerald Sigmund's apartment house.

Thirteen minutes later, he kicked the building door open and hauled an armload of Siggy's fine-looking audio equipment out to the Porsche. He dumped it on the floor on the passenger side, and swung back for more. The next three trips, he schlepped out clothes. I wished I could have gotten him to strap Siggy's big flat screen HDTV to my hood, while he was at it. The final time, he came out with a couple of lidded plastic shoeboxes and locked them in the trunk. I didn't know what was in them, but I knew what wasn't. Harold and I had scoured Siggy's apartment and hadn't found any drugs, cash, small animals, firearms or stray computer discs.

George wasn't as methodical as Harold when he left Siggy's place. He didn't even glance in my direction as he made tracks for Hertel Avenue. It crossed my mind that Siggy wasn't dead at all, that he was pulling an elaborate hoax, and George was bringing him clothes and things. Then the Porsche did a U-turn and slid to a stop in front of Chickie's Pawn Shop. He popped open the trunk and carried the shoeboxes inside. I left my car at a meter across the street and took a huge, huge risk. I strolled in to see my friend Chickie.

The door buzzer pinged as I walked in. "Bella Santini, as I live and breathe! How you doin', sweetheart?"

"Hey, Chickie, it's good to see you." His real name was Chester Vecchio, and he'd been on the Buffalo PD organized crime task force with Pop for as long as I could remember. Everybody called him Chickie. When I was little, I asked Pop if it had to do with barnyard animals. My father just winked. Now, Chickie ran a nice little enterprise buying and selling merchandise he hoped – but couldn't guarantee – wasn't hotter than the proverbial two-dollar pistol. The rest of the time he was in Pop's basement working over the cold cases, drawing diagrams and making notes until he ran out of ink. George Cabral twisted around when he saw me and fumbled a shoebox, dumping Siggy and Norbert's fancy watch collection all over the linoleum.

I took a pre-emptive shot. "Don't I know you?"

Before he could answer, Chickie asked me what I needed. I told him I needed to win the lottery, but in the meantime I could use a decent acoustic guitar. I knew from experience that he'd be fresh out. He always said nobody gives up a guitar or a wedding ring without a lot of sadness, and he wouldn't have them around. Lord knows what that was about. But he caught my drift and played along.

"If you can wait till I'm done here, I'll check the back," he said. Which meant I could watch Cabral truck in everything he stole from Siggy and Norbert. I told Chickie, while Cabral was out between trips, where the loot had come from. Chickie waited until Cabral had brought it all in, then told him he couldn't use any of it. If he'd bought it, he would have been receiving stolen property. Plus, as Siggy's case progressed, he would have forfeited whatever he'd paid Cabral, when the cops figured it out and confiscated the goods.

I busied myself with fake Mont Blanc pens and Rolexes until Cabral, blowing smoke out his ass, heaved all the stuff back into the Porsche and left to try another pawn shop. I didn't bother to follow. I knew everything about him I needed to know. He was a small time hustler. The only thing that bothered me was how he'd gotten into Siggy's apartment. I gave Chickie a kiss on the cheek, handed him the Porsche's tag number and description and went outside. I knew he'd be on the phone to Robbery, before the door closed.

But how *did* Cabral get into Siggy's place? On a hunch, I dialed My Apartment and got lucky twice. First, Damian didn't answer. Second, Honey was very preoccupied in the dressing room, getting ready for her closeup, and she didn't have a lot of time to chat. "Honey, I'm really sorry to bother you. But I was wondering if you still had the key to Siggy's place, and whether I could us it in the next few minutes to have another quick look for those story notes." Of course I'd made a duplicate key, but she didn't know that. I just wanted to see if she still had hers.

"Ummm, you could borrow it, but I lent it to this guy."

"Oh yeah? Another reporter from our station, George Keele?" I made up the name, but threw in George to get her started.

"No, a different George. He's not a reporter, just, ummm, a friend." Bingo. Translation: Hell hath no fury. My loser boyfriend just jettisoned me so he could poke another guy... so here, help yourself to all his worldly possessions. I had to tell Vicky about this. She'd love it.

But exactly how much was Honey capable of? I let her get back to her Special K, which reminded me of breakfast, which reminded me of lunch. Right after, I'd stake out My Apartment.

I was rolling down the street past Buffalo's closed-down churches and open bars, with visions of fried chicken and biscuits dancing in my head, when my cell rang. It was the newsroom. There was a hostage situation on the top floor of an Erie County satellite courthouse.

Some idiot husband named Shale Opat had seized a Deputy's gun during his divorce hearing in Courtroom B, and was holding it to his wife, Katrina's, head. This was on the fourth floor. He'd have to scoot down four flights of stairs – or ride an elevator – past every sheriff's Deputy in Erie County, to get out of there. They would not be amused that he'd swiped their buddy's gun. He didn't have a snowball's chance in hell. And what could he possibly hope to achieve with this? "Let me stay married to you, honey, and I won't shoot you?" Yeah, that makes him so much more appealing. It's my personal opinion that any man who pulls shit like that just confirms that the woman who left him was right, he *is* a freak.

By the time I got to the courthouse, the building had been evacuated and the crowd was fidgeting behind yellow crime scene tape. The police department had thrown up barricades across the streets, but we had gotten lucky, because our live truck had already been set-up for the noon news. We were allowed to stay inside the secured zone, behind a gazillion patrol cars with lights flashing and enough hardware to arm a small banana republic. But nobody, not even us, was allowed any nearer the building.

It was four stories of brick and stone, with a set of steps up to heavy carved oak doors under a homey, old-fashioned clock. I wouldn't have minded walking barefoot on the cool lawn, and rolling around in the shade. Just knowing that I couldn't get to the water fountain, or even the bird bath, made me hotter and really thirsty. That, and imagining the salty breading of the nice fried chicken I'd be eating if I hadn't answered the phone.

I left the car two streets over, hopped the barricades and hiked up to the truck. Smitty, my photographer and friend from the old days, was waiting. I hardly recognized him, he'd lost so much weight since he gave up smoked sausage and beer. He'd always been real sensitive about the poundage. He had the tripod and camera set up so that we had a perfect view of the main entrance, just behind me. If Opat tried to shoot his way out he'd probably use that door. Plus, if he chose the one on the south side, it could be in our camera shot with an easy swing of the lens.

Smitty handed me the microphone, and propped up a seven-inch television just below the camera. That would be my monitor, so I could see what was on the air. I'd be able to tell if my hair was so out-of-control it was making sheepdogs jealous. And which one of us was on camera, the anchor in the studio or me. Also I could see if we were rolling video while I was talking, making it safe to do stuff I'd never want made public...like fish lint out of my nostril.

I plugged my earpiece into the monitor, and listened for the control room and the anchor's mike check. The public information officer at the sheriff's department – the PIO – would be my best source at this point. Good PIO's know this, and they float from one news crew to the next, ready to do interviews. It's their fifteen minutes of fame. The rest of the time, they're either backing off comment on some important story, or taking us to lunch as a consolation prize. I tucked my hair behind my ears and checked it in the reflection of the camera lens. Smitty counted me down.

"Ten... five, four..." he switched to hand signals, and we were on the air. The PIO told me what he knew, which was damn near nothing. Except for a few tidbits he'd picked up from a law student who was asleep in the back of the courtroom during the hearing, and then hit the gates when Shale Opat charged the Deputy.

Katrina Opat had been on the stand, a diminutive Hamburg farmer's wife of about fifty, with a dry, lined face and thin blondish hair pulled back with bobby pins. Her hands clasped in the lap of her flowered cotton shirtwaist dress, she told the judge how Shale had chased her with a hunting knife out by the barn, and damn near sliced her. Shale looked to be in better physical condition than his wife. He was sunburned and pumped up, with the body mass of a 22 cubic foot Maytag side-by-side.

"How did she get away?" I asked the PIO on camera.

"Gave him the slip under the cows."

"What was his motivation? Why was he after her?"

"Well, they hadn't been getting along too well, goes without saying. She told the judge it was his snoring, mostly. And passing gas extra loud and extra long when her mother visits. Anyway, along comes the County Fair, and they're both getting ready for competition. He signs up for Animal Sciences, and she signs up for Cooking, like always."

"And what, he didn't like her cooking?"

"Oh, he usually does. Katrina fixes a mean Welsh Rabbit."

"And?" Geez, it was going to take pliers to pull the story out of him.

"Welsh Rabbit doesn't have any meat in it. Usually. But this year she called hers Shale's Surprise Welsh Rabbit. Surprise was, it had chunks of Flemish Giant in it."

"That would be a mushroom?"

"That would be a bunny. Mr. Opat's prize-winning rabbit. Took first place last year. That's when he got out the hunting knife."

Just then, a shot rang out and I did a half-twist dive for the truck. Smitty beat me to it and shouted back, "Don't run. Don't let him know you're scared!"

"*Bull...shit.* Outta my way fat boy!" My motto is live to fight another day.

Nothing else happened for ten minutes, so every reporter and cameraman within a hundred yards hand-and-kneed it out from under cars and vans, like slugs after a rain. Then a Deputy shouted that the round had come from the second floor hallway. The media shifted into overdrive, everybody talking at once: "Pull back! Get a shot of the door! Not that one, damn it, *that* one! He's coming out!"... "I don't give a rat's ass, break into the freakin' soap opera. Get me on *now*!" In the slow motion stillness of gathering my thoughts and waiting for my cue, my eyes scanned the spectators... and I spotted him.

Harold. At the edge of the crowd, on the other side of the barricade. His eyes were trained on me, focused, waiting for me to notice him. He was composed, in a real executive-looking long sleeve white and grey pinstripe shirt and yellow tie, hands in his pockets. To everyone else, he was probably just another courthouse employee, or maybe a lawyer waiting to get back inside. He looked like he belonged. Harold's smirk said he knew I couldn't go after him.

"How much time?" I snarled at Smitty.

"Thirty seconds. Out of a commercial break."

"Okay, control room, listen carefully," I said to the crew back at the station. "This is an emergency. Get *somebody* to make a very fast phone call." I repeated Daly's 800-number three times, and told them to say Harold was in the crowd. I hoped they wouldn't blow it off. Smitty was counting down the last ten seconds. I made a *mano cornuta* with my free hand and poked it a few times at Harold. Nonna swears those horns deflect the evil eye, and launch a Karmic asskicking.

"Stand by!" Our anchor, John Miller, had thrown it to me and I was on the air, a tight one-shot, while Harold calmly watched. I took a deep breath and tried hard to erase the murderous look in my eyes.

"John, it appears Shale Opat has left the fourth floor courtroom. We still don't know exactly what has happened inside, or whether anyone has been hurt. At least one shot was fired moments ago, apparently in the second floor hallway, and it's possible Opat is looking for an escape route."

I have no idea what else I said. All I could think was that one shithead was keeping me from chasing another one, and I wanted to crack their heads together like walnuts. Miller and I talked back and forth a few minutes, recapping what we knew. The PIO saw we were live and strolled over, but it turned out he didn't have anything to add.

I had just thanked him for his non-update, when the air around us exploded with cracks of gunfire. Opat burst out the front doors. He had a shrieking woman in a chokehold, lifting her off her feet, while his semiautomatic blasted wild rounds into the trees and pavement. He was probably handier with a knife. He reeled down the steps, blinking, surprised at the crowd and unsure of where to go. One of the cops yelled that it was Mrs. Opat he had. My eyes swung back to Smitty, who had taken root behind the camera, and then back to the other side of the yellow tape, where Harold had evaporated into the amusement park wave of commotion.

"Damn it, damn it, damn it! He was right here, and now he's gone to ground again! Damn it!" I stomped so hard my heel put a dent in the tar vein running through the pavement.

"Who?" Smitty and the control room asked in unison. No time to explain. Back at Loser Husband Central, Opat and his hostage wife were on the move. The police had been ordered to hold fire. Sharpshooters were itching to take him out, but Katrina's legs were an eggbeater, and her movements were pushing him all over the map.

I turned back just for one more second, squinting into the sun, trying to scope out Harold. Smitty kept an eye on the action, as he'd done a million times. But he'd never been transfixed, making little peeping noises before. I whipped back. Opat, now directly behind me, had put the gun to Katrina's head and was picking up speed. He was hauling her through the line of police cars, straight over to us. Our eyes met. He rotated his gun uncertainly, midway between Katrina and me. Opat was a crazed hulk, but I was a very angry, fire-breathing woman. That wife-abusing bastard had just cost me Harold!

I jettisoned the mike toward Smitty and hurled myself at Opat. Once we connected, I knew what Daly meant when he said to go for it, because an attacker will expect defense, not offense. I clamped onto Opat's wrist and jerked his gun upward, off Katrina. He was so shocked, he let loose of her. Then I grabbed him by both shoulders and dug my nails in good and tight. It felt fabulous. I launched my knee so far into his crotch, he was choking on pubic hair. He dropped the gun and bent over to grab for his privates, and I latched onto his head like a football and used my knee again to thwack his nose up into his teaspoon of grey matter. The big guy dropped solidly and didn't move.

At that point, a smart woman would have retrieved his gun, or what the hell, let the cops take over. But maybe it was reaction to what had happened at My Apartment, or rage at Opat, or Harold, or abusive men in general... whatever triggered it, I was sitting on him, drilling his face with my ring hand, until they finally pulled me off.

"I... am... impressed," Daly whistled low, studying me cooly. "Remind me never to piss you off."

"That son of a bitch..." I stammered furiously, suddenly aware of police radios and of poor, terrified Katrina blinking down at her sweaty, whimpering husband. Her toe nudged his shoulder gingerly, half expecting him to come to life and bite it off. "You go, girl," I growled. "*Divorce granted.*"

"Ahem, we're *still live*." Smitty laughed from behind the camera. "And may I say, welcome back."

On the walk over to the car, I couldn't help evaluating my on-camera effort, it was the natural thing to do. Informational content: the best that could be achieved. Hair: okay. Wardrobe: questionable. Never wear black slacks when you're going to straddle a maniac in the street, wear something pavement colored. On the positive side, I was glad I hadn't skimped on the underarm shaving. Entertainment value: priceless. Whether I found Siggy or not, after this I was getting a bonus from Soper one way or another. We sat in the Toad, where Daly looked completely out of place. Forgettable automobiles are not his style. I checked to make sure Daisy was still holstered on my ankle. Daly glanced at his slacks, too.

"Ha! Everything there?" I asked.

"One of us should take inventory."

I was slowly coming down from my second adrenalin rush in a week of near-death moments, and it was dawning on me that we all could have been killed. But we were alive, and it felt good. So good, my hand slid over to the bulge in Daly's pants. He covered it and pressed down. Hard as a rock, and the size of my hair dryer. Was it his closeness to me, or was it the danger? "Is that a 9 mm in your pocket, or are you just glad to see me?"

"What do *you* think?" he said as we kissed, and he closed his fist around my hair. Every part or my body was screaming *Me first*!

I never could trust my hands. They were squeezing his gun like day-old bread. It took my lips twenty seconds to decide opening them to his tongue would feel good. Little Janis was working up a healthy blush. He was doing recon of my breasts through my shirt, and my nipples thought being tweaked by his nails was the most fun they'd had all day. Which was a special treat for a bunch of fifth grade field trippers, passing the car on the trek back to the school bus to write "What I Learned

On My Visit To The Courthouse". It was the first time I'd seen Daly even close to embarrassed.

When I told the control room to call him, he was already at the scene, watching the crowd – and Harold. But Harold wasn't stupid. He'd also seen Daly, because Daly was the only other person whose attention was not focused on the courthouse. Harold knew then that he was under surveillance. By whom, didn't really matter. When Opat came out shooting, Harold simply melted into the chaos. He was good. Our boy had gone pro.

Tango pulled out Honey's home address. "We could tail her together," he said.

"Honey who?" I sighed. And I knew that with my body calling the shots, we'd never get any work done. What would be more important? Finding out what happened to Siggy and possibly stopping a murder, or rolling around in cool sheets on a muggy summer afternoon with one of the few charismatic, sexy, straight, single, non-smoking guys left in the world? The answer came easily.

But I said goodbye to Daly anyway, and put the car in gear. I called up the number for My Apartment, which by now was on one-touch dial, and a hundred-year-old woman answered. Maybe somebody had gone too far with the hormone shots. She said Honey had the day off. So I found Honey's house on the map and headed for Delaware, then cut across to Afton, on the lower west side.

I cruised a block past Honey's place, did a showy Lovejoy High Driver's Ed k-turn, and eased up to the curb. The street of red clapboard homes had changed hands, and ethnicities, many times since the Italians came in a century ago. These are telescoping houses. One in front, a smaller one attached behind it, and then another, even smaller one. The driveway can go all the way to the back, with an off-ramp for the first garage. You could squeeze in a lot of taxpayers that way. Honey shared a neglected two bedroom fronthouse with another Rockette. A life-size ceramic Labrador puppy sat placidly by the mailbox guarding the overgrowth, wondering who stole the mower.

If Sweet Boy had been with me, I could at least have pulled a wig and sneakers out of the trunk for a disguise. Now the best I could do was wrestle my hair into a scrunchie. I covered up with a baggy turquoise station t-shirt, turned inside out so the logo didn't show. As if having an orange cotton candy pouf stuck to the back of my head wouldn't draw any attention.

Somebody's grandfather was sweeping leaves off the walk two doors the other side of Honey. A block further down, teenage boys were fooling around in front of a mini grocery. The place just this side of Honey was home to William and Slava, according to the sign by the door. Slava was on her knees putting in new flowers next to the Mary-on-the-Half-Shell. That's the Polish answer to a grotto, a statue cradled inside a clawfoot tub buried so that just one end is above ground. Slava gathered up her tools, struggled to her feet and went inside.

I left the car and hugged the opposite sidewalk. No activity at Honey's, and no car in the open garage. Open could mean somebody was coming back soon, or they just left. I owed it to myself to get a peek through the window. I was halfway across the street when a shiny new, pale pink T-bird sailed around the corner, testing the laws of gravity. And I understood how squirrels feel. *Stay or go? Stay or go?* I hustled back to the sidewalk and plastered myself up against a splintery creosoted utility pole, and got very quiet. The T-bird did a creative maneuver into Honey's garage. Good, she was home. I ambled further down the block toward the boys. They stopped playing grab-ass long enough to determine I wasn't going to bust them for anything. I crossed to Honey's side, and doubled back.

Thirty feet to go. I was a bundle of nerves, but doing okay. Then Renza's white Taurus rounded the corner on two wheels, and slid to a stop in front. *Holy Mother of Pearl! Heart attack city!* I froze, then dived into the bushes where the old man had just swept. He did a double take through his screen door, went away and came back out with his glasses on, and checked again. About that time, we both jerked around to see Renza hop out of his car and go inside.

The old man peered at me, waiting for an explanation. I fished twigs out of my hair, buying time. Odds were he and the go-go dancer were not close friends, I couldn't see them spending evenings popping open brews and comparing notes on neighborhood meetings. I could say Renza was my cheating boyfriend, which was sort of true. Or admit I was an investigator, or a reporter. I chose the first one, whispering pitifully that Renza was my fiance', and now I knew the horrible, sordid truth. He waved me off. Through the screen door, the volume on Gilligan's Island cranked up.

At this point, an investigator worth her salt would be photographing the cheating bastard through Honey's window. But all I could think was *Idiot!* Just two days ago I'd fallen for his beignets and bare skin, and now look! Johnny Renza, my perpetual mistake, was hooked up with a stripper. This would not look good on his resume'. I re-crossed the street and skulked back to the car. Before the door swung open, I risked an honest self-appraisal in the window. All due respect, I did look like a bag lady. And Honey looked, well, beyond hot. Which was more appealing to a man? Even my dad had an opinion. I slid down in the seat to chew on the steering wheel, and dialed Vicky.

"*Balducci's Love Your Dog*, ya got Vicky here."

"Vicky, come take my gun or I'm going to shoot him."

"Which one?"

"Renza. I'm outside Honey's hovel, and he's inside."

"Inside what?"

"My point exactly. What the hell's he doing in there?"

"Janice, best friends will always manufacture something to make you feel better. How's this... he's workin' on a story."

"Yeah, the story of my ass."

"Alrighty then," Vicky said. ""Let's change the subject. Sandro's here."

"Sandro's where?" I asked, fearing the rest. She had the jewelry of a Mafia princess, but I could never see her with hair teased that high.

"He's staying with me."

"Staying, as in staying? But why?"

"Cause he's interesting, in a *consigliere* sort of way, and very sexy. I'm smiling so big I could eat the phone."

"But why now, after all these years? I mean, he's a sweet guy and he's my cousin an' all, but they don't call him The Eel just 'cause his clothes are slippery. Vicky, he *is* slippery."

"I know another reason he's The Eel. The man's dick has been to dancing school. Huh uh, I'm diggin' in. If he wants to get rid of me, he'll have to toss me out a window."

"Sandro *lettered* in window tossing!" But it was too late. Vicky was doomed to a life of thick black eyeliner, and Sunday barbeques with the squalling kids of goons with names like Razor, Shark and the Clip. "But he lives in Jersey, and you live here," I pointed out. "You wouldn't move and leave me with this cluster fuck, would you?"

"As it happens, The Eel is about to swim into our waters. Some arrangement between the Families, that's all he'll say."

"Get used to it," I told her. "Sandro absolutely never talks about business. His mouth is shut so tight, his dentist has to pull a knife just to check his teeth. A call's coming in. Gotta go."

It sounded like a screaming Italian carpet warehouse commercial. Pop was grappling for the handpiece and there was a lot of scuffling. Then Nonna Giovanna landed him one square in the chops.

"Pommie!" he bellowed in the background, "your grandmother's knockin' out my teeth!"

When it comes to brawling, Nonna doesn't play fair, and she absolutely never, ever loses. "Shhht. Shhht," she hissed. "This family's go-

ing right down the *pischadoo*. Pommie, your mother got busted at poker!"

EIGHT

"MA BUSTED AT POKER?" Nonna must have got it wrong. "Put Pop on."

"Not yet. Listen, we need a sit-down about this. You want I should lean on somebody? Such a marvelous opportunity to make a classic statement." Her vocabulary was meshing nicely, I thought.

"Nonna... put... Pop... on...the phone!"

"Sheech," she blew out, and handed it over.

Pop's voice was evening out. "Your mother was playin' an early game at St. Agatha's, and all hell broke loose. It's dat damn text messaging. And Giulia Giuliani. Dere still fightin', those two, an' it's time to hang up da gloves." Ma had talked her poker-playing geriatric splinter group into getting their grown kids to buy them cell phones. They could do it cheap, on the family plan. That way, the girls could stay in touch during the games. Only the games were played for real money, which kind of took them from amateur to professional. The priest caught Ma messaging Rita Bogucci about two aces she saw in Giulia's hand. Giulia was Ma's nemesis. In the last millennium, she stole my mother's first love, Radicchio, bragged about it for weeks, and then dumped him. Ever since, Ma has looked for payback. Today, she'd tried to throw a cash poker game to get it.

Pop's voice went up an octave. "Somebody dialed 911 and Shaky had to respond. He couldn't just ignore a call." Shaky was Dussel Cargone, a friend of Pop's. He got the nickname from the only time he'd ever discharged his weapon in the line of duty. He'd jumped in on a 7:00 a.m. convenience store hold-up. The perp turned around and squeezed one off in Shaky's direction. It was a whistler... it literally cut a swath through his Bobby Darren pompadour.

But the plot thickens. He'd been known to enjoy a nip or twelve when he went off duty, and the night before the holdup had been a twelver. He was real hungover. The security camera tape showed him firing back, trembling like Jello, juggling his gun with both hands aiming somewhere around the guy's knees. At that point, the robber reached for the sky and started sobbing. He figured with Shaky on the trigger, the odds of losing the family jewels were greater than getting shot through the heart.

"So where's Ma now?" I asked Pop.

"Down at the station. I'm goin' to get her. Meet you there?"

"See you in ten."

I swung the car around in a squeal of rubber, and left cheating Renza and Bubble Dancing Barbie in the rearview mirror. "I'll get to you later," I yelled out the window, "and your little dog, too!"

My mother in jail. There were days when we all wanted her there, but when it came right down to it, how dare they! What could possibly have happened that would justify locking up the best lasagna cook in Western New York?

Pop rolled into the lot right behind me. I jumped out and hit the ground running. He about yanked my arm off, and smiled. "Relaaax, Pommie, nice an' easy." Wider grin, slower walk. And then I got it. "Wanna cuppa coffee first?" he asked. His eyes twinkled and shone the way they did when they'd watched me unload my little Christmas stocking off the fireplace mantle. "As long as we're all home in time to eat dinner." It was tempting to cool our heels outside for half an hour, but in the end we relented. We went inside to the duty desk and sprung my mother from the slammer.

"What's she in for?" Pop asked Shaky.

The five-foot-six Johnny Walker Red flask adjusted himself and answered, "Assault. And assault on a police officer. Violation of charitable gaming law. Oh hell, it's a little unclear. There are conflicting stories. The assault happened between her and Giulia Giuliani, so that's a crap shoot. But when she flipped me off and then stuck that same finger in my eye, that was assault on a police officer, and I had to do something. She'll walk today, okay, but it won't be that way next time, *capice*?"

Ma appeared in the lobby, looking shaken but not stirred. She carried herself like Queen Elizabeth, her white plastic pocketbook hooked over her wrist. Without a word, she lifted her chin so high she could hardly see over her nose, and marched right past us out the door. We were still doing double takes when she reversed rudder and came back in.

"I have a message for you," she stage-whispered to me, "from somebody on the inside of the Big House. One word: Honey." And Ma left again.

Pop hit the traffic lights better than I did, thanks to decades of practice, and beat me home. I caught up with them in the kitchen, where my mother was already putting on the pasta water and opening cans of tomatoes.

"What did you mean by 'Honey'? Who said it?" I asked her.

"Shhht. Shhht. A woman of the night," she pronounced, as she chucked empty cans into the sink. "We talked. She knew you. Something about being there when you got an education. Did she go to the U? Was she in your class?" Ma dropped the last can and gave me a look.

"What. What? Say it!" I hated when she gave me the look. I turned to Tony, who had tucked himself in the corner by the back door. He mouthed *Ma knows*.

"I'm saying nothing, Pommie. Except you should get married again. Don't wait until it's too late, until you forget how, and then you have to fend for yourself," Ma said, reaching into the salt box.

"I *am* fending for myself. And I do it really well!" I could not have this conversation one more time. The rest of Ma's information told me nothing. She didn't know the woman's name, and could barely describe her. She could be anybody.

"Humph." Pop retreated down the basement stairs into his cold case office, and made some calls. Twenty minutes later he was upstairs with her name, Sharilyn Farrell, along with copies of her various mug shots. Her pose was improving. I suppose there's an art to it, if you get enough practice.

"Five bucks says you recognize her," he said to me, "and not from college."

I couldn't be positive, but I thought I knew her from the dressing dive in My Apartment. The spiky-haired brunette in the tangerine bikini and black sequin choker. Not an altogether unflattering look. So she turned tricks, too. I had a flashback of Renza going into Honey's house, and wanted to scream.

I vibrated outside to the front steps, and got Daly on the phone. "Guess what, one of the erstwhile dancers at My Apartment is a hooker."

"Is this a joke? Are these Italian girls?" he asked.

"No, really. Pop gave me her name. She was in the can with my mom, I'll tell you about that later." Daly was silent. I had the feeling he was re-evaluating his assessment of me as an intelligent woman.

"Janice," he said flatly. "Of course she's a hooker. They're all hookers." Of course they are, Janice. Did I really think they could support themselves and their various close encounters with controlled substances on what they made at that bottom-rung dive? How can I be a kick-ass woman of mystery, when I call Daly with something so ridiculous?

"It's okay. You know there's more to it," he said. He was right. This puzzle had lots of pieces, but I couldn't put them together without his help. So I told him about Renza visiting Honey, actually going where she lived. I could hear the jealous gears between his ears grinding through the scene of sin at my apartment. The breakfast leftovers on the table, the post-sex powdered sugar on the floor. And now the same guy doing it with a whore. What did that make me?

My finger spelled out "slut" in the dirt on the top step. "So what are we going to do?" I asked optimistically.

"We?"

"Please. You *said* you'd help."

"I will. But I like it when you beg. It's the sugar on my beignet. Who's the broad your dad dug up?" I gave him the rundown on Sharilyn Farrell. Then he got my hopes up, when he said his contact at the forensics lab had left a message for him to call ASAP.

A hot breeze was kicking up, and the sky looked like rain. My sinuses were so plugged, it felt like somebody was sitting on my head. Ma had moved to the stove, to sauté garlic in the big pot. "Have some," she said, "it cures everything."

"Ma, promise me there isn't going to be any more trouble at St. Agatha's. You're not going tonight, are you?" I asked.

"Darn tootin' I am. But I'll leave Officer Friendly out of it. Shaky's a good kid. His eye just walked into my finger, that's all." My mother turned to Tony. "Son, put out the flamingo." He'd changed out of his white cable company shirt into something more Tony, a grey tee that said *What, no f****ing ziti*?

He frowned. "Ma, I love you like a mother, but the flamingo's buried till next week. Let's not tempt fate." He wasn't kidding about the buried part. All our lives, the only way we could ever have any secrets from her was to literally bury them in the back. When we ran out of space in our own yard, we made deals with friends.

"Atsa right!" Nonna cruised in, resplendent in the new crocheted black shawl that had just arrived from QVC, along with an updated black rayon dress with pleated shoulders from HSN. "Now is not the time to stir the waters. No flamingo. But you gotta show at the Executive Game." Her voice took off like an SST. She had my mother nose-to-nose by the blouse collar, her chest heaving. "They may not like you, but they *will respect* you!"

Pop ever so gently patted Nonna's shoulders. "*Maddone*. Okay, Mom, it's okay. Margie got da message. Turn her loose, now."

Geez, the drama. Tony had tried to get Nonna interested in *I Dream of Jeannie* instead of mob TV, but she couldn't get the hang of Jeannie's little head bounce. Hers was more *grand mal* than grand magic. Then too, Jeannie's version of making somebody disappear and, say, Janice Soprano's, were as different as day and night. And Nonna just naturally took to the night.

I left with a half gallon of red sauce and two freezer bags full of fresh meatballs, along with Pop's faxes of hooker highlights. My thoughts ran amok, connecting the dots. Balls....hooker....*Renza*. I found a Kleenex and blew till my ears rang. Next thing I knew, the Toad was idling in front of Renza's house on Herzog, a scant four blocks from my parents. It didn't look like he was home. He could be doing a live shot on the evening news, or out cruising in his stealthmobile. I rolled down the windows and dug in. This was as good a night as any for war.

Three hours and fifteen minutes went by. I know exactly, because I didn't piddle before I left Ma's, and every ten minutes I was thinking about relieving myself in his backyard. I reached around for another meatball... that made thirteen. The urge got stronger. I couldn't use the coffee can I reserved for peeing on stakeouts, because whoever was driving Sweet Boy had it. I prayed they'd get real thirsty and fill it with drinking water. I dug around in the console for a napkin, and came up empty. Desperately sucking tomato sauce off my fingers, I made for a clump of hydrangeas in Renza's front yard. From there, I could dash unseen to the back. Unfortunately, my body didn't get the message.

My slacks came down just ahead of Niagara Falls. At which point Renza's red Camaro pulled into the drive. He peered into the dark, and left the motor running and the lights on as he crouched in a low run across the lawn. I ripped up a fistful of grass to wipe myself, but Niagara was still falling and everything got soaked. Renza saw it was me, and doubled up laughing. He crawled over to the hydrangeas for a closer look. This was not the position of strength I had in mind.

"I thought it was a family of raccoons," he snorted. He went inside and let the dog out, then turned off the car and came back. By then, I was zipping up. Little Janice was itching and mad as hell about the grass, which smelled like it had been sprayed with something chemical, maybe weed killer.

"I can hardly wait to hear it," he said as he popped open a Golden and handed it over. "What's your bush doing in mine, and why is there spaghetti sauce on your zipper?

"Shut up!" This was a disaster. How can you humiliate a man for his trashy behavior when your pants are wet and his dog is gnawing at your crotch?

"No, Thumper, down boy!" Renza pulled him off. Thumper belonged to Renza's uncle Vinnie, and looked like he'd been whupped with an ugly stick. His lanky yellow body had hair in only three places: his ears, his chin, and his you-know-what. He stayed with Renza whenever Vinnie was drying out, which was monthly. Vinnie's place was a microscopic clapboard over on Vienna. Mrs. Vinnie had solved the space problem thirty years ago, by moving out. Vinnie solves it by sitting on the front porch with his best friend, Jack Daniels, watching the 10:05 a.m. Norfolk Southern go by. And the 11:50, the 3:20 p.m., the 9:55 and the 4:00 a.m. Which has led to his status as Lovejoy Drying Out Champion, seniors division.

Every month when his disability check rolls in, Vinnie and Jack celebrate. Jack waits on the shelf in the liquor store while Vinnie cashes the check at Finance Bank, where his cousin Francine is assistant manager. She always keeps some back. Then Jack and Vinnie go home together. When the last bottle is empty, Vinnie flops on the curb of the police station and passes out. He sleeps it off in an empty holding cell. It costs the taxpayer nothing, because Vinnie doesn't eat while he's hibernating. Four days later, Vinnie and Thumper drift by Francine's to collect the rest of the money for groceries and doggie biscuits, until the next disability check, and the cycle starts again. Obviously, Thumper is not a dog of means. His bags are always packed. He got his name doing what he was doing right now to my leg.

"Tomato sauce drives him wild," Renza said.

"Better than Honey?" My excellent comeback was completely wasted. Renza gave me a blank look and popped one open for himself, while we watched Thumper download on the lawn. When he was finished, he loped back up the steps to pick up licking at my zipper.

"Don't lie to me, Johnny, I want to know what you're doing with Honey Summer."

He choked on a mouthful and shifted around. "Hell, Janice, you go right for the bottom line, don't you?"

"I wanted to go for the throat, but one slapfight a day is my limit."

"Yeah, I heard about that. You really cleaned Opat's clock. He could've wasted both you and his wife, you realize that."

"Don't change the subject," I said as I guzzled some more. I couldn't explain my weakness for cheap beer on front door stoops with cheating lovers.

"Same as before. Can't tell you. Except that it's purely professional. I'm doing a series and she figures into it. You have to trust me." He patted my knee. I imagined him doing that to Honey, and bored my nails deep between the tendons. He yipped and my mood improved.

I told him, "You better do better than that."

"Hey, *you* were following *me*."

"No, I was tailing Honey."

"Why?" he asked.

"None of your business. Where'd you meet her," I asked him, "at a literary lecture, or maybe a scientific symposium?"

"She goes to the same day spa as a friend of mine. Star Luxury, it's called. You know, for the crap you girls get done. Massages, Brazilian waxes, stuff you don't want us to know about." My mind re-racked an imaginary tape of Honey motioning toward every fuzzy little girl down there, where her skirt ought to be. Why did I always pick guys who were so much work?

"Whatever's on your mind, nothing like that's going on with her," he said. "She's important to my story, and her place is just the safest place to meet. Period."

While I thought that one over, I made him give me back the Stickie notes I got from Siggie's office, just on general principles. He hadn't given me one teeny bit of information in return. I had to win *something* tonight.

"Why should I believe you about Honey?" Here we go again, his hand was back on my knee. The indentations from my nails were turning satisfyingly dark.

"Because she's not my type," he said low, drawing out tyyyyype. He focused on my lips, teasing them with a slow rub of the thumbs. If I sucked just once, would that be bad? His hands felt cool against the slow burn of my cheeks. He whispered, "How could I ever be with someone like her, after you?"

Made sense to *me*. I shook my head till it rattled, then handed off the empty beer can and sprinted over to my car.

"Hey, don't kill my shrubs! You can always go inside!"

I flipped him off sweetly, and gave him an eyeful of the Toad's tail lights. It wasn't until I crossed the tracks that I realized he'd slipped one past me. Some other woman, some "friend", was close enough to him to talk about Brazilian waxing her whutzis, and I didn't ask who. See, that's why Renza's so dangerous. You never know if he *means* to make you forget, or if it's a natural gift.

The attraction of the rebel kicked in the day I watched Sister Superior chase him down to cut his hair. It was cinematic. Her robes were flapping and her supersize rosary beads were hissing as she gained on him, but he was laughing and running like the wind. What style!

What attitude! Of course, eventually he got clipped. Everybody knows you can't outrun nun shoes.

I was glad when I got home, where things were what they appeared to be, and life was uncomplicated. I chucked what was left of the meatballs and sauce in the freezer, tossed my slacks in the dry cleaning pile and drew a hot, bubbly bath. The phone rang just as I was arranging Hershey kisses and red wine in a neat little row along the top of the tub. It was Daly.

"Hang onto your hat," he said.

"I'm not wearing one. Or anything."

"On second thought, this news really ought to be delivered in person."

"Too late. There's a chair up against the door, and I've got a gun," I said.

"Breaking in would be completely unnecessary, sweetheart. However, did you ever install ratchet bars on your sliding glass doors?"

"On the *sixth floor*?" I asked.

"That's what I thought. So here's the latest: The forensics lab has been having trouble with the DNA tests on the finger. In the process, somebody realized the blood hadn't been typed. Guess what, it isn't Siggy's."

"Isn't Siggy's blood?" I asked, mystified.

"Isn't Siggy's anything," Daly said. "The gift in your desk doesn't belong to Gerald Sigmund."

"But I was with his own brother when he identified it. He ought to know! Now, of course, Harold's hiding." What was it that had made Harold so sure? Then it hit me. "It's the ring," I told Daly. "It has to be the ring. But it looked like a gay pride ring." Although I couldn't really see Siggy narrowing his options with the ladies by wearing something that would alienate an entire gender, it was possible. Love's a fool's game.

"You're right. Lots of men could wear the same one. I'd put Norbert Dojka at the top of that list. Hang on, I'm going to put you on hold."

If he was right, that'd blow Longoria's theory about Leonard Halley right off the map. And open a million other questions. He came back on the line..

"We need to start thinking in terms of who has *the best opportunity* to control an operation on a day-to-day basis. Call me if you need me," he said, and the line went dead.

I dropped the phone on the bathroom counter. *If it wasn't Siggy's, then whose was it?* I sank up to my chin in the tub. With a gut full of meatballs, I looked four months pregnant as my stern finally settled on the bottom. But it should have been more fun. There was no way I could stare down a glass of red wine now, with all that blood in my head. The chocolate, however, worked wonders. Until I heard Harold's voice in the living room.

"I know you're there. Tsk, tsk. Messy situation for your mother today, she ought to be more careful," he said as my answer phone screened his call. "Messy pants for you tonight. Can't you Santinis do anything right?"

I jettisoned out of the tub and skated across the soapy floor to the phone. "*Who is this?*"

"You know who this is."

"Harold? I've got to talk to you. Where are you?"

"No."

"Then what do you want, why are you calling? How do you know about my mother?"

He exhaled a disgusted breath. "You're not the only one with connections. And I know everything you do. I don't want you to find my brother anymore. And you'll never *find* me. So drop it before somebody else gets hurt."

"Who? Who's going to get hurt, Harold?" The phone was slippery and I fumbled it, ripping my thumb nail right into the quick on the edge of the counter. "Damn it! Harold? Hello, Harold? You still there?" He sniffed a couple of times to let me know he was.

I tried the low, threatening tone I used to get store refunds without receipts. "Harold, who else could get hurt? Don't go, I have something to tell you." He was deliberately breathing loudly enough for me to hear. Then he hung up.

Bathing had lost its appeal. I felt exposed. I grabbed a towel and wrapped it around me, getting all goosepimply and scanning the ceiling. Harold knew everything that was going on. He was a computer freak. He'd bugged his own apartment, why not mine? Normally I wouldn't call Daly back when I was naked as a jaybird, because I was pretty sure he'd know it, and then I'd know that he knew it, and then all that knowing could get out of hand. But nobody could locate bugs the way he could, and it couldn't wait until morning. So I took the phone out on the balcony and dialed. If you're going to sweep, you don't want to announce it in the target area.

He was there thirty seconds after I hung up. By then, I was dressed in a ratty old t-shirt and jeans, and felt like forty miles of bad road. Odds would be better than average that I wasn't going to throw myself at his feet and try to pick up where we left off in the car. The odds were wrong.

The man looked mysterious and inviting, the way the night does, in a midnight blue track suit and matching running shoes. A big, brown leather duffle looked promising at his feet. If the neighbors thought he was spending the night, they'd be talking until next year about what could have been in a bag that size.

"You rang?" he said, and strolled in. "I'm struck by the irony. Here we are, your place at night. No broken down door, no glass in your head. Just you, fresh out of the bath, all dreamy and relaxed, and me..."

"What're you, high? I'm jumpier 'n James Brown channeling the Dallas Cowgirls."

"Shhhhh, beautiful." He put a finger to my lips, then to his. I knew the drill, it had just never been done in my own home before. This was not a routine bug check. We would play the game until we knew for sure if Harold was eavesdropping. Small talk only... what a nice surprise to see you here, how's the weather, what's in the news, etc. Obviously if Harold could actually see us, the jig would be up. What if both Harold and Siggy were watching, laughing?

All Daly's equipment is computerized. The analyzer works with the laptop. It's very sophisticated and I don't understand any of it, which is why Daly's the one doing it. He swept the entire apartment for audio, then video. He turned on the hot water in my bathroom sink and waited for the big mirror to fog. No round, fog-free spot on the mirror, which meant there was no camera on the other side. Normally, he'd hold his thumb nail against mirrors that were firmly fixed to inside walls. If the nail meets its own reflection with no gap, its a two-way mirror. Cool.

And he took the phones apart. I love the old fashioned ones with cords, because they make me feel like a screen goddess. They give my apartment the illusion of being filthy rich, as opposed to just filthy. Unfortunately, those simple phones are also the easiest to tap. He pulled paper clips out of two of them. Next, Daly produced a gizmo with eight flashing red LED lights. In the middle there's a viewfinder, like a gun sight.

"Refresh my memory," I asked him. "You point the side with the lights toward the suspect area and look through the sight. Then what?"

"If a camera is there, the curve of the lens reflects the red light back at you, and bingo, you can see it. That's especially useful when you have to do this in the dark. Bad guys like to wire the camera to the lights for power, so it's only operational when the lights are on," Daly explained. "That way, they don't have a running recording of twenty-three hours of useless blank tape. If we were to have the lights on now, they'd eventually check the tape and know we're on to them."

I followed him like a puppy into the bedroom, and he caught my hand before it reached out of habit for the switch. "We'll work in the dark. And remember to keep your hands to yourself." I pinched his fine butt to let him know I'd heard.

He opened a couple of dresser drawers and let his fingers swim around in my silky undies. I could feel him studying me in the dark. Oh sweet Jesus. "Which ones will you wear tomorrow?" he whispered.

"Tomorrow I'm getting a mouse trap for that drawer."

"Huhhhh," he said as he closed it. His vibrations were bouncing off me like waves on a stormy shore. I felt drunk.

The flashlight beam canvassed the room. It came to rest on an especially dusty part of the polished walnut dresser top. My maid had departed – along with the only really bitchin' corset I ever owned – when her checks started bouncing. Red satin with black trim, from Frederick's of Hollywood. And real metal garter clips, not that soft plastic crap. Now that I did my own cleaning, I liked the efficiency of dusting off bedroom furniture with my panties on the way to the hamper... when I thought about it. Hence, dust thick enough to write in.

Daly eyeballed the ceiling directly above. "It's not what you think," he whispered, as he climbed onto a chair and aimed the detection apparatus toward the tiny dot of a pinhole camera, as it began reflecting flashing red light. Harold was good, but Daly was better. He noticed Harold hadn't cleaned up after himself when he drilled the ceiling holes, that's why it looked like heavy dust.

On countless nights in that bedroom, I'd fantasized Daly would whisper to me in the dark. And he now he was doing it: "They're in, times three. One's a looker." He was telling me he'd found three bugs, and one was a camera. He turned the television in the living room up loud, and pointed us out into the hallway. "Camera in the bedroom, sorry about that. What can I say, he has good taste. Audio in the kitchen and bathroom. I disabled the phone taps, which had turned the telephones in the living room into full-room microphones."

Camera in my bedroom, camera in my bedroom. My heart dropped into my socks. Harold had watched me dress... and undress... and other stuff, the slimy bastard. He'd seen me rub *Cellulite Be Gone* into my Italian thighs in front of the closet mirror, and practice Victoria's Secret runway poses in leopard push-up bras. And suck in my belly till I nearly passed out. And dig one-size-too-small thong underwear out of my ass. Unfortunately, except for that, there was less action in my bedroom than anywhere else in my life. I didn't want Daly to know that.

"I'll check the utility closet by the elevator, to see whether he's storing the stuff on tape," he said, "or whether he's burst-transmitting it out digitally at a set time of day. Either way, beautiful, you've got a problem. But... and *it's a huge but...*"

"What? Huge butt?" My head was still back in the bedroom mirror with my thighs.

"I said, your place is bugged, *but* if you can make him think you don't know, we can feed him disinformation and force a move. Can you do that? Control what you say in there for a couple of days?"

I have never controlled myself for longer than it takes to work the ribbon off a box of Godiva truffles, but I said okay. "What about the camera in the bedroom?"

"Wear a robe in the bedroom until the lights go out. Then mess up your bed and go sleep on the couch. Quietly. Or stay at my place, that would work." He gave me those innocent you're-safe-with-me eyes. And I knew I was. And I definitely wasn't. We said we'd meet for coffee in the morning to map out a plan.

He was inside collecting his gear when the phone rang. It was Margaret Segal in 5-A, the apartment just below. The ninety-year-old Gladys Kravitz of Eric Towers was a retired federal judge, and always had her finger on building security. "Word up," she warned, "a cop just followed Ingersoll, in 5-B, into the building. He's on his way up to see you." I dragged Daly over by the television to whisper it to him. Then we raced around collecting equipment. He was stashing the last of it in the coat closet when the knock came.

I yanked the door open. Longoria. He was looking more and more like Dracula. "Why Frank, what a surprise, you here at midnight. Lose your cape?" It was too easy to needle him. Of course he could slam me into storage at a moment's notice, so maybe I should back off.

"Happened to be in the neighborhood. And look who's here," he said acidly, taking in Daly.

"Detective." Daly wasn't any happier to see him. It was more than professional jealousy. Cops think private detectives are amateurs, and private detectives think cops have too much latitude. Truth is, PI's have to accomplish twice as much to be considered half as good. Daly and Longoria despised each other for reasons that had piled up over the years. Longoria was a dangerous enemy, and Daly knew to tread lightly. This didn't come naturally to a man who had more professional covert experience under his belt than Longoria could ever dream about in his flannel jammies at night. If he ever decided to come after Daly, he'd have to find him first – and then, there'd be a few surprises.

Longoria pushed his hat back, and chewed his gum like it was two in the afternoon. "Mind if I come in?"

"It's late. What for?" I yawned big.

"Well, now..." he half closed his eyes and winked at Daly, cracking little bubbles, making a cheap male joke. Daly's engines were screaming like an Airbus, but the brakes were full on and the chassis was shaking.

Longoria loved it. If Daly lost control and tore into him, Frank would have the excuse he'd always wanted. "Hear anything new about Gerald Sigmund?" Frank asked. That sounded a lot like bait.

"No," I told him. "Have you?"

"Don't expect to. Halley hasn't sent a ransom note to Soper, or to Harold. He clipped Siggy and carved his finger strictly as a one-time get-even. He knows he'll be caught. We've verified he never left town."

Daly stood with his arms half-bent, hands almost touching. I knew his body language. Good martial artists don't fold their arms when there's a chance they might need them. It adds an extra two seconds reaction time. He said to Longoria, "You still dead sure it's Gerald Sigmund's finger?"

"Naturally." Longoria shifted to shoot me a pretty damned intimidating look. "Miss Santini, here, was with the brother when he ID'd it... weren't you, dear?"

I rolled my eyes. Daly couldn't lay a hand on the cop, but he aimed his words like knives. "Speaking of fishing, Detective, how do you explain the deceased's note that said 'Gone fishing'?"

Longoria was ready. "A bluff, written under duress. Halley made him do it, to buy time."

I was getting fed up. Why was he lying? I figured he'd take it for granted we'd already heard the finger wasn't Siggy's. And I was dying to confront him on ignoring the wirecopy he'd taken from me. I hated this fooling around and opened my mouth to say so, but something made me glance at Daly. He was giving me an imperceptible shut-the-hell-up.

"Don't worry," Longoria smirked. "Good detective work stays on track."

"Self-satisfied little shit," Daly said in the hallway when the elevator doors closed on Longoria. "Here's what we learned: He doesn't know about Harold's bugs in here. If he did, he wouldn't need to ask questions, he'd just listen in. Now about Harold: If his equipment isn't picking up everything that just happened in real time, whenever his transmitter does feed him audio from your bathroom, he'll hear you taking my call tonight. And then he'll see we know about the DNA test. He ought to be thrilled that the finger isn't his brother's, but something tells me that won't be the case."

After Daly left, I made a big show of pulling the blackout drapes in the bedroom and pretending to sleep, pondering whether Longoria could actually be too stupid to keep digging for the real answer. Then I crawled into the living room and tossed around on the sleep sofa until it got light out.

At dawn's early crack, I crawled back in and threw open the drapes just for show, in case the damn camera over my bed had another power source and it could see without the lights on. The whole thing was ridiculous.

I rattled around in the kitchen and put on some coffee. Liberating the Stickie notes from my purse, I assembled them like a crop circle on the table. Renza never did say whether he'd learned anything from them. Then I opened Siggy's note to the news director, and planted it in the middle. Girls, sex, drugs, just your average day in Siggy's life, only he wasn't there. His note stared back at me. *Gone fishing. Babbo.* I brought some java back to the table and waited for the caffeine to kick in. The more I thought about it, the more this whole thing smelled like a rat. The kind of rat that packs heat and says Yo. So I called in an expert.

It was 9:00 a.m., and somewhere in Buffalo – I tried hard to imagine it was not in Vicky's bed – Sandro smoothed back his hair and flipped open his cell. "Speak."

"Oh, I'm sorry, is this Johnny Sack? I'm looking for Sandro DiLeo."

"Heyyyy, Cuz. I talked that way a long-o time-o before the *Sopranos*, who were able to acquire it from me. What's up?"

"A confidential question," I said.

"Is there any other kind."

NINE

ALL JOKING ASIDE, WHICH is not easy around Sandro, it can be beneficial to have a connected relative. Of course, with Pop always yearning to bust his balls and having to hold off for the sake of the family, over the years a lot has gone unsaid.

"I've said too much already," Sandro told me on the phone.

"You've said nothing. I still don't know who's only pretending to be a cop. I know lots of officers, and as far as I can tell, they've all been to the academy." I ticked off the list: Kielbasa, Longoria, Frasier, assorted patrolmen including Wolenski, all of Pop's friends.

"Let me put it another way," he said. "When a cop is *not only* a cop. Think about it. Meanwhile, what else is new with the mystery digital."

"You mean digit."

"Yeah, whatever."

I told him about Siggy's notes. "He said the same thing in both the message his girlfriend found in his apartment, and in the one that was mailed to his boss. *Gone fishing. Babbo.* What do you think? He's not a fisherman, unless you count trolling for the lowest forms of life late at night in places the rest of us don't go."

"No shit. Fishin'. Babbo. Articulate Babbo," he said, so I spelled it. "Whoa. You don't got a live one, you got a dead one. He made somebody very angry. He's whacked, definitely whacked. And somebody thinks it's funny."

"But why? For what?" I asked. It wasn't that hard to believe a person would want to clobber Siggy, no doubt there was a waiting list. "I always thought it'd be uncomplicated. Some drugged-up, jilted girl with a cleaver looking to give his skull a sunroof. Or maybe an angry husband peeling off a long shot with a Sniper Scope."

"Not that I would have any personal knowledge of the terminology his friends might utilize," Sandro went on, "but Babbo is Obbab backwards. That's a jerk who has shit for brains. He has outlived his usefulness to a certain cadre of unspecific individuals. Individuals who might have interests-in-common with said corpse. To say he has gone fishin' is to suggest that by now his socks are soggy, and somewhere downriver a carp is crapping his jewelry. *Capice*?"

I asked Sandro if he was sure, and he told me I could take it to the bank, and hung up. "Okay, Harold," I said into the dead phone as if the loser could hear, "I know where your brother is, and I'm not telling you."

Truth was, I had no idea. Exactly where do you look for a wet body in a city on a lake?

I poured coffee into my insulated Buffalo Sabres travel cup, and took the elevator down to the garage with no particular destination in mind. More than anything, I wanted my own scanner so I could hear emergency channels. Police divers, for example. Payday, I was buying one. The news department had one. I could alert the newsroom, but to what? Plus, if another reporter found Siggy before I did, I wouldn't get the money. So who could I ask for help? Kielbasa, maybe. But if Ma heard I was over to see him again, she'd be asking him to dinner and sifting sugar on pink and white engagement pastries. And she'd put those little silvery balls on them.

I shoved the seatbelt clip home, wondering when my life was going to straighten out. The mug was almost into the cup holder, when the passenger door jerked open and a figure fell in beside me. In absolute panic, I couldn't remember a single move Daly had taught me. What was that elbow strike thing? Bend your arm, turn your fist, rotate it down and swing. "*Oh mama, my pants! That's hot!*" Coffee was everywhere.

"Aw geez, Pommie," my father said, "how many times do I gotta tell you to lock da car as soon as you get inside?

"Inside the *car*? How'd you get inside the *garage*?"

"It's not rocket surgery. If I can do it, imagine who else can."

Upstairs, I tried to soak Colombian French roast out of new white cotton pants that would never turn it loose. "So what're you doing here?" I asked Pop. "I mean, it's great to see you, but you're hardly ever over."

Out of habit, his eyes probed the room over my shoulder, looking for god knows what... stray men? Freshly ironed twenties? I laughed, "Want to pat me down while you're at it?"

"Did that when I was changin' your diapers. So tell me, when was da last time an exterminator was in?" He was talking about two-legged pests.

"Last night," I whispered as I put a finger up to my lips. "You and Ma have a fight or something?"

Pop looked distracted. "Don't be ridiculous. For that to happen, I'd have to get in a word edgewise. I came because some things can't be said on the phone."

"You telling me your phone's tapped?"

"A long fax is comin' in, and da secure line's tied up." Pop might have put together a damn solid cold case cracking gang, but on retired cops' income, one extra phone line is the best they can do. I put on fresh coffee. He poured a merlot. At eleven a.m.

"Cocktail time in Palermo. "Let's go outside."

On the balcony, we watched confused low clouds bounce off each other in the wind on the lake. The sun was high, and when the clouds parted we sizzled like rotisserie chickens.

"I'll make this quick," he said. "Word is, one Gerald Sigmund's been found. And he don't look good."

"Meaning?"

"Da boy's been takin' on water worse than your mother after a salt herring supper."

"Is he... dead?"

"If he ain't, he's doin' one hell of an impersonation. They're draggin' him out of Smokes Creek as we speak. Couple of bass fishermen hooked him this morning. Personally, that don't seem like prime bass water to me. I've had better luck at Burt Dam, but it's a good hike up dere."

I flipped my coffee, cup and all, over the balcony and took Pop's wine glass. When it was empty, I went in and got the bottle. To speculate with Sandro about mob-style killing is one thing. To find an actual waterlogged, puffy body is something else. "Does he have all his... you know, all his fingers?"

"Let's go find out. I'll drive. Da wine was for you anyways. You passed the legal limit half a bottle ago." He checked his watch. "And it took just under thirteen minutes." He steered me toward the door. "Bring those," he said toward my sneakers.

Pop pointed his oversize navy blue Ford Fairlane south on Route 5, and made for Lackawanna. The car was older than dirt, but in mint condition. It was like driving your living room.

"So how'd you find out?" I asked him, watching the pavement blur.

"Your law abiding cousin, Sandro. Said he just talked to you. Wanted me to be the one to tell you, so you didn't go flyin' over to the Precinct without a plan. I called Tall Drink, an' he confirmed divers are down." Tall Drink Nylan is a giant, hairless teddy bear who stands about nine feet, from the ground to the top of his glossy, shaved melon. He's a friend of my father's, still working. So Sandro had read the signs right. By the time we located police vehicles and hiked over to the water, half a dozen cops were standing around the body. It's always struck me how quiet the scene is, when everybody knows there's no emergency anymore. You rush to get there, and then there are no lights, no sirens. Also, in this case, no Frank.

"Hey," Kielbasa came up behind me.

"Hey, Leon. What's goin' down?"

"Your reporter friend." They'd put the body in a bag, but hadn't zipped it yet. He was mushy and bloated and pasty, but still sort of looked like Siggy. Only smaller, not so formidable. I stared at his chest for a long minute, expecting it to move. Zowie, if it did, I'd be outta there.

"You do a finger count?" I asked, right before I hurled in the weeds. In a week, I'd turned into a one-woman projectile epidemic.

"You were throwing up last time I saw you, too. You could get a reputation," Leon said, reaching down to pull at the side of the bag. "See, I already checked. All ten. And looky what's on one of them." Siggy's right middle finger was swollen around a gold ring. Exactly like the one in my desk drawer.

"Where's the big detective?" I slobbered, as Pop dabbed at my face with Kleenex.

Harper Frasier tapped me on the shoulder. "He sent me." Harper was even cuter than I remembered outside Longoria's office the day I handed over the wire copy. Maybe I'd miscalculated in high school. I'd been down with such a case of Renza Influenza, I'd overlooked the possibility of dynamite teenage irresponsibility with Harper. And now we were past it. Harper was a grown-up and I was... I was standing in a field with my daddy fishing spit out of my hair.

Longoria had bailed. Why? This was his own high-profile gig, sure to get his face on the tube. Maybe he was home rehearsing his ad-libs. Or maybe he *didn't want* to be on television. I checked my phone for bars, to call the story in. And of course, to tell His News Directorship that I would accept cash or check as payment for locating Mr. Sigmund.

That was when a uniform shouted, "Detective Frasier, you might want to have a look at this!"

"This" turned out to be a second body. Siggy had company down there. I didn't recognize this one, but he was minus a little something, the right middle finger. My guess was it was Norbert. The cops wouldn't speculate on the cause of death, but everybody agreed they hadn't accidentally fallen in. Both had been weighted down with chains and cinderblocks, and the job looked very pro.

Waiting for the live truck, I dabbed on under-eye cover, powder, lipstick and eyeliner. And perfume, don't leave home without it. I got on the phone and read the rules again to my cheapskate employer, who wanted to renegotiate terms.

"Show me the money, all of it," I told Soper. "If my photographer doesn't show up with a check for a thousand dollars with Pompeo Santini written on the front, go fish." Heh heh.

The live truck left the road and didn't brake, as it bounced over a low bluff. We had maybe ten minutes' lead time before other stations would show up. Smitty was waving the check out the window. I galloped toward him and snatched it. "Heads up," he shouted, "Soper's looking for another ratings spike. He's offering twice this much to the reporter who comes up with Siggy's brother."

"That would be me!" I said gleefully. In truth, the chances weren't great. While I could never find Harold, he could always find me. On the other hand, just when I thought I'd never find Siggy, look how *he* showed up.

While Smitty was setting up by the water, three other news vehicles were closing distance behind him. "Stand by and stand back," I shouted at them. "Let the big dog eat!" I reeled in Kielbasa by the belt loops, and Smitty tossed me the mike.

In the sixty seconds before air, I flashed the check in front of the camera and blotted my lipstick in a big kiss on the back. "All contributions gratefully accepted," I said as I tucked it down the front of my shirt.

Smitty was counting down. "Five... four... three..." then he went to hand cues. The station hadn't had time to round up an anchor and get one on set, so this would be all me, breaking into the regular programming.

"I'm PJ Santini with this *exclusive*, breaking story. The body of investigative reporter Gerald Sigmund has just been recovered from the waters of Smokes Creek, near Lackawanna. This story is developing and details are coming in as we're reporting them to you. With me now is Buffalo police sergeant Leon Kielbasa. Sergeant, what can you tell us?"

The camera hung on our two-shot, as Leon began to fill in the time and location. Then it panned smoothly past us, to the divers and the first body bag. He explained how the fishermen had been chilling in their boat with a twelve-pack and a cooler of sub sandwiches, when they got a hook caught on what they thought was a tire. They were going to cut line and try a different spot, when it occurred to them tires don't usually wear shirts. So they called 911. Divers were deployed to go down and retrieve the bad news. Smitty brought the shot back to us, and I asked Kielbasa about the second body. There weren't many details yet, but he maneuvered nicely around it and we all looked like we knew what we were doing.

"Thank you, Sergeant," I said when he wound down. Other reporters, who basically had no story without him, were shooting me daggers while they waited. But I don't like sharing my men, even if we're only talking, so I smushed his toe into the soft dirt and he had to stay. He didn't complain. All in all, it was a calm, confident, dare I say award-winning few minutes.

Turning back to the camera, I recapped the story. "We'll bring you more on this breaking news as it becomes available. Reporting live from Smokes Creek... what the hell?... *Ho-ly Smokes*!"

Nonna Giovanna, who should have been home arguing with Ma about dinner, appeared out of nowhere and rushed the camera shot, wrapping Leon and me in a truckload of billowing black chiffon.

"The *bischero* got whacked, I knew it! He sleeps with the fishes, and now you're safe. This is the biggest value of the day!" She danced as she launched a blizzard of dried herbs into the air.

"No, they didn't find Harold, this is Gerald... what're we even talking about?" I said, coughing up rosemary. She couldn't do this to me. My masterpiece, my *piece de resistance*, was still on the air. I took blind, frantic swings to clear some breathing space, and connected with Mamie Kilebasa, knocking her flat off her feet.

"Mama!" Leon squeaked. Kielbasa's five-foot bowling ball of a mother was on her back in the dirt, flailing around like a fat black beetle with car keys.

"Leon, my child, I brought a meal. Help me up, I'll get the mustard."

"This is... was... PJ Santini..." I moaned into the mike, "whatever... *but it was a damn good story, and you heard it here first*!"

When it was all over, when the Coroner's wagon had taken the bodies away and the other news organizations had finally stopped laughing, I found my father slumped in the front seat of his Fairlane. He lifted his head off the steering wheel and tried to focus. "I'm so sorry. I thought we were safe because she couldn't drive."

He reluctantly took Nonna Giovanna back home with him, and I retreated to the station, riding beside Smitty. On the way, I mentally scratched Siggy's window-dressing roomie, Norbert, off the suspect list. And, what with the cement blocks and twenty pounds of chains wrapped around the two bodies, it didn't look like Honey had done it, either. Or maybe she just didn't do the heavy lifting.

A lot more on the story had to be worked up for the evening news. Until then, through the magic of magnetic tape they could replay my original report. I racked my brain and fabricated ten creative ways to finish the story without having to show my face in the newsroom. But none of them was good enough, so I shook the herbs out of my hair, hiked up my purse and swung around the corner. Three reporters, the weatherman and even the intern froze in their tracks.

"What," I said. "What? You act like I'm a grenade somebody just threw in."

"Way to go, Janice." Renza jumped up. "You did one hell of an excellent job. Congratulations." He pumped my hand. I didn't know how to take that, coming from the guy everybody knew had pumped everything *but* my hand since I was in a training bra.

"Yeah, especially the finale." I'd know that simper anywhere. Kathy Shula was hunkered down behind his computer, fluttering her eyelashes.

"*She's* batting falsies that look like mosquitoes are trapped on her lids, and you're staring at *me*?" I said to everybody in general. Kathy adjusted her pink lace top, and checked the powder blue teddy that hiked-up her twin peaks. Real professional.

"Um, Soper did ask me to update her on the system," he said.

"Yeah, I bet. More like she's updating you on *her* system. Reminds me," I told Renza as I blew back out into the hallway, "you really should do a series on prostitution." He turned fifteen shades of red.

I slammed my door. It was almost three. If there were no snags, I could get everything written and pre-taped by 5:30. If they needed a live update for the 6:00 news, I'd do that too. By 6:30, I could be stretched out on my balcony with a dirty martini, ordering Chinese. I put in a call to Homicide and left a message for Longoria to please favor me with an update, which of course he didn't. Kielbasa called and said there was nothing new, it was too early for autopsy reports, and anyway Longoria was the one who'd go on record with that. So I used what I had, and wrote it up every imaginable way, so I could get the hell out of there.

My mind was bogged down with Sandro's word puzzle: When a cop is not only a cop. I unlocked my desk and pulled out a bulky envelope with *In Case Of Emergency* scrawled on it in red. I carefully unwrapped a 97% cacao bar. Inside of six chews, the answer came: A cop is *not only* a cop when he's also a card carrying mobster. Both Sandro and Pop had said there was a mob connection, so why couldn't it be a cop. But who? Who had another master to serve in this particular investigation? Could be anybody. He had to be found.

But not tonight, not by me. 6:30 rolled around just like it was supposed to, and so did the good General. I lined everything up on the dining room table... the chicken, the healthful fat-free steamed rice I should eat, and the pork fried rice I was actually going to eat. I cracked open the chopsticks, heaped a plateful and settled down to flip through channels. The station was running *Desperate Housewives* back seasons. Nicollette Sheridan's character, Edie, spat out, "I know who she is. She's a man-eating, scum-sucking ho-bag!" And all this time, I thought Kathy was my own special problem.

The show went to a commercial break, and I settled back. Insolent saxophone music over a black screen gave way to a dreamy blur of crimson movement. My kind of evening. When the camera focused, it was on a woman's feet strutting in skyscraper, ankle strap, fuck-me-red heels. The voice was deep and masculine. "Sex for sale. The Buffalo you don't know." Men with their faces obscured knocked on the doors of ordinary-looking houses on simple, pretty streets. They walked right in. The music morphed into an unsettling staccato. "Join reporter John Renza, as he goes behind the scenes to reveal Buffalo's out-in-the-open sex trade. Don't miss the first installment of *The Prostitute Next Door*. Tomorrow night at six."

The shock of it sucked a chunk of chicken right down my windpipe. I had to Heimlich myself! Mental note: *When a table is just right for sex, it's too low for Heimlich.* When my chest finally connected with a corner of the table, the General shot out of my mouth and ricocheted off the screen. Not three hours ago, I'd stood right next to Renza and he'd said zero about this! But I was right on, wasn't I, when I told him he should do a story on prostitution. Okay, so what did this mean? It meant he was *miles lower* than a snake's belly, and I called to tell him so.

He didn't answer. I didn't leave a message, and immediately regretted unblocking my number. I'd wanted him to know it was me only so he'd answer and I could tell him off.

Twenty minutes later, he was at the door. "You rang?"

That was it, I burst into tears. "Can't I control *anything* about my life? For Chrissake, how'd you get past the doorman this time?"

"My secret," Renza said.

"You've got too many secrets. Go away."

"Now, now, sweet thing, at least let me explain," he said as he planted himself on the couch. I let him go on, while I scooped up all the food and plopped it on the kitchen counter. The last thing he was getting was my Chinese. He said he'd promised Honey he wouldn't discuss her involvement in his series, or her identity, if she'd agree to be interviewed. I got that, but that wasn't the real issue.

"Oh please," I said. "Protecting her identity means disguising her voice and her face, we all know that. But if interviewing was all you two were doing at her house, where was your cameraman, in your pocket?"

"My photog is a she, and she was late. When you follow somebody, PJ, don't give up and leave so soon." That really deflated me. Renza found my remote and began checking channels, as if he lived there and the discussion were over. I grabbed it and shut it off, greedily licking sweet-and-sour sauce off the volume button.

"I wasn't following you," I said, "I was following *her*."

"I know. She said you'd been over to My Apartment. But just now was the first I heard about the fight."

"It wasn't a fight. Who told you?"

"My contact at the cop shop just called to rip me a new one. He's wound up about the series, says it blows their investigation. But then he wanted to know what's up with you and the strip joint. He says the ever-present Tangy Daly brought you in to file a report."

My back started to itch. "Tango's just a friend." I reached around to scratch lower.

"See how tight you're wound? That's why I've been keeping an eye on you. That was me tailing you from the station, Monday night."

My heart skipped a beat. "You mean, you were worried about me?"

"Course I am, you nutcase. You shouldn't be driving around alone at night. But then, your buddies Smith and Wesson were with you, weren't they? You can still smell the fumes in the hallway."

"It's a Sig. Do you have any idea how hard my heart was pounding in there? Worse than the field trip to the museum, junior year." The Iron Island Museum is in a really old Lovejoy building that started out as a church, advanced to a funeral parlor and now is the official guardian of the past. Until it wound up on *Ghost Hunters*, hardly anybody would admit it was haunted. I, on the other hand, had nightmares for a month after my class went through. I will not go in there again.

"I guess I misjudged you, Johnny, I don't know what to say." I felt like a real heel.

"You can tell me why you're interested in Honey. You told her you wanted her keys to get Siggy's work papers out of his apartment, but I don't buy it. You've got an office filled with his crap. I saw you throwing it out." He stretched like a cat, and spread his hands behind his fine neck. "You still don't trust me, do you?"

"Frankly, no."

"Okay. Here's what I'm going to do. I'll give you something nobody else has, give it to you on a silver platter."

"What, your datebook?"

"Better," he said.

My radar went up. "Like what?" I asked, reaching for a chopstick to fine tune my scratching technique.

"Direct from the source: Leonard Halley's been picked up. He's in jail. Go with it. It's yours." Now, why would he do that? He did look sincere. "Go do it," he said. "You'll be the first one in town. While you're at it, ask Longoria what his theory is *now*."

Renza even insisted on taking me over to the station and waiting through the whole thing. I phoned Homicide to get confirmation. Sure enough, Halley had been arrested at Jake's Hideway with his girlfriend, Yeulah Hilroy. Skulking flat on his ass under the bed, with his leg in a cast, high as five kites on Percocet. Said he broke it during escape from custody. That checked out. He could not possibly have kidnapped or killed Siggy or Norbert, or anybody else. As usual, no statement from Longoria.

As Renza and I headed back to my condo, I mulled over the shrinking list of suspects. I wasn't surprised Halley wasn't on it. I *was* surprised when Renza pulled up in front of my building and let me out. I felt the tiniest twinge of regret that he didn't even try to come upstairs.

Sleeping on the couch wasn't the exotic escapade it had started out to be. It amounted to camping out on an expensive cot. I spent a good part of the night wondering what Renza had done after he dropped me off, if he had a late date. I shuffled into the kitchen at dawn, flipped up the lid on the coffeemaker and started pouring in water. It occurred to me I could be a Freudian freak, hooked on the drama of never knowing what the man was thinking. But why would I need that, when I was having my own adventures all over the place?

Damn it, pay attention! The lid had come down and I was still pouring, mornings not being my prime alert hours. I mopped up with Wei-To-Go napkins and hit the ON button.

To get my mind off Renza while I was waiting, I invented an imaginary butler named Simon. "Simon, please tell Monsieur Café I'm awake. And bring some nonfat yogurt. Hershey kisses for dipping? But of course." I was just licking Dannon off the chocolate, when Daly called.

"The diner. Bring your gun. Holster it high."

I would've poured a cup while I was dressing, but I'd forgotten to put in the coffee.

I threw on black slacks and a thin cardigan with little pearl buttons, from the stack by the door. Thanks to that bastard Harold's cameras, I still couldn't walk around undressed in my own bedroom. I saw that as lost independence, so to compensate I left four buttons undone. So sue me.

Omelet's Diner was mid-morning empty. Two iced teas were sitting on the table. "You don't have to tell me to carry my gun, you know, I always do. I just can't always get to it."

"You start now."

"I'm safe when I'm with you," I said.

"You're not always with me." He was looking incredibly cool, for a man so hot. Whenever we were together, he could possess me without touching. I wondered if he knew that.

He leveled those dreamy greens at me. "You keep thinking that way, Janice, there'll be no going back." *Who wants to go back?*

"This situation is developing," Daly said. "Two bodies, no firm answers. Except Honey's playing a bigger part."

My thoughts exactly. I filled him in on Renza's series, and how Honey was one of those 'prostitutes next door'.

"A good beginning," he said. "But think back to My Apartment. They'd only just begun working you over. When did everybody back off?"

"They just stopped. Honey walked in."

"Exactly. Honey walked in. It's her show."

"Tsh. That's impossible, the girl's an idiot!"

"Even idiots are good at something," he said. "She controls what goes on. Somebody else handles the dollars, and I think I know who.

We're going to that hole you call an office." He pulled out his wallet and dropped a crisp twenty on the table. When a diner is your second home, it's smart to keep the staff happy.

"I'm feeling pretty stressed. Any chance after this I can borrow your BMW for about an hour?" I asked him.

"No."

"How come?"

Daly made a face like he'd heard it all, and took off down the road. I dialed him up.

"Why not?" I asked again.

"Because I know what you want it for. Because, Janice, you can't park by the side of a busy road and point your black hairdryer at passing vehicles. Someday somebody's going to drive into a light pole."

"But that's my deep dark secret! How'd you find out?"

"I not only found out, I have pictures. You should have worn a hat. I heard from two cops. One thought it was hysterical, he said it looked like a clown had escaped from a mental institution. The other cop is waiting for you to do it one more time. His list of charges is too long to go into."

"That's not fair! I'm relieving stress while I perform a public service by keeping people from speeding! Right? Hello?" We cruised into the lot in silence.

Saturdays are pretty quiet at a TV station, so it was easy for us to slip in unnoticed. I'd very attractively duct taped the wall switch in the on position, so we actually had some light. Daly knew exactly what to go after in the computer, and took all of ten minutes doing it. Siggy's email was riddled with messages to Harold, in a vernacular that wouldn't make much sense if you weren't looking for clues. It was the jackpot, the gold mine everybody was looking for.

Coded emails detailed working names of prostitutes, customers, services rendered and dollar amounts. High buck VIP's included at least one prominent city council member and two popular clergymen. Even my plumber was on the list. I was definitely paying him too much.

"I got C's in math, but this I can add up. It's got to be a million dollars, and all cash," I said, "not counting the obvious extortion potential."

"It's the other half of what you found on Harold's computer... they're linked. From here, you can go to the days of the week in his Favorites, see? It's entirely possible there's nothing on paper about any of it. Harold obviously doesn't have access to the nuts and bolts himself, he just set it up and handles the cash. Siggy did it all from here, or at Harold's."

"So it's not like somebody lifted stuff from Siggy's apartment before I got there. There *never was* anything there. Harold didn't know that, so he hired me to get the key and steal the logins and financial books."

"Exactly. The drug connection has to be here, too," Daly said. "Costa Rica."

All this time I'd been concentrating on finding one missing person, when right under my nose, Harold had a giant prostitution operation to protect. "But why is he so frantic about it," I asked Daly, "if the only other person who knows how it's run is Honey? I don't care what you say, she's got the smarts of a rock. She's nothing to worry about."

"Harold's not just racing Honey. His real competition is much more powerful. Which is why I want you to carry your gun, lock your car as soon as you get in, and pay attention to your rearview mirror. I'd tell you to leave the rest to me, but I know you won't. So," he waited a beat, then said what we both knew, "if anybody has kept any records at all, it's Honey. You two still need to talk."

I drove around in circles, making phone calls, working up to it. She wasn't at My Apartment. So where would a long-haired, long-nailed, long-legged twenty three-year-old be, if she had lots of money and every fuzzy little girl down there needed attention? Star Luxury, of course, for one-stop shopping.. I got Vicky on the phone as the car closed in on her shop. "Yo, Filomena, you're getting your nails done. I'm right around the corner."

"What's with the Yo?"

"Ha! With Sandro as your bunkmate, there's going to be a lot Yo-ing going on. You and the little yo-yo's."

"Who talked to you? How do you know this?"

"Know what?" I asked.

"I think the bastard's knocked me up."

The Toad jumped the curb at Balducci's, and my feet did not touch the ground. "What, are you sure?" Visions of tiny, dark-haired shiny-suited babies with goatees were dancing in my head. Vicky was in her lab coat, bent over an Irish setter. She turned, and I tripped when I saw it. Thick black eyeliner. Double hoop earrings the size of espresso cups.

"I'd get that stuff off before I leave the building," I said.

"Oh. You obviously are not acquainted with the intricacies of applying facial adornment. It is an art." Vicky had undergone a complete transformation. Her hair was still long, straight and blonde, but it reached to the ceiling.

"Why're you talking like that, and what truck did those twelve gold chains fall off of?"

"The Sandro truck," she sighed. "He's a sweetheart. You gotta run me by my place first, I want to show you something."

"Okay, but when we get to Star Luxury, take the gum out. Nobody'll believe it."

When two people are stone cold sober, car time is the only time you can get a straight answer, because nobody can leave. So I grilled her. How could she know she was pregnant by a guy she just started dating? She owned up to a teeny indiscretion out in the tool shed last month during Sunday dinner, somewhere between the meat and the dessert. I bit hard into my bent knuckle.

"Well at least you're still independent enough to have your own place," I said as we swung open the door to her apartment. "Oh my god, what happened to the furniture?" The living room looked like Madonna had thrown up all over it.

"This is what I wanted to show you," Vicky said.

"But where's all your single girl *Sex and the City* stuff?"

"That isn't really Sandro's style."

"What *is* Sandro's style?"

Vicky swung over to the shiny white sofa and slid down the arm onto a seat that expressed air like a whoopee cushion. "Leather, baby!"

"There's such a thing as crinkle burnout patent leather?" I asked.

"It's new."

"It's impossible. Why does the coffee table have a little brass sign screwed into it that says *Non Smoking Room*? And where'd he get a television that takes up an entire wall?"

"I know. We have to stand out in the hall to watch. Life's a gift, my friend, ride it like you stole it. Anyway, I needed a change and he's good to me. Look, we're taking a high-end vacation!" The glass table top was littered with travel brochures.

"Atlantic City? Vegas? You said high-end. I was thinking Paris, Rome."

"Sandro knows some people. It'll cost practically nothing. He says we can't lose."

"I bet."

The bedroom had gone from classic oak to off-white, all of it. Including a dresser with a dazzling display of pinkie rings of every description, and Sandro's gold neck chain with an Italian horn.

"He's got this thick nest of chest hair," Vicky swooned. "I love running my nails across it. When he's naked, I don't know whether to jump him or groom him."

"He do a lot of calling?" I asked. There were five identical silver cell phones.

"He has one for everything."

"Ever peek at the numbers?"

"Janice! I'd never look! Anyway, the keyboards are locked."

"If it's so private, how do you know they're locked?"

"Oops."

This relationship had so many flashing red lights, you needed shades.

"I know what you're thinking... hang on, I'm gettin' ready," Vicky said as she broke the seal on a giant tub of lip gloss, "But see, Sandro's really very easy going. For instance, he forgave me for wrecking his sports car."

"What? When? Are you okay?"

"Not the outside, the inside. It really wasn't anybody's fault. I had this litter of sweet Golden retriever puppies to take over to the vet for their six-week shots. They were all curled up sound asleep in a cardboard box, and I thought, why move 'em into a travel kennel? So I put the box in that little place behind the seats. I'm making good time goin' up The 90, when they wake up and raise hell back there. They're jumping up and hooking onto the ceiling cloth with their sharp little nails and shredding the shit out of it. Riding it down like a surfboard, the way cats do on curtains."

"That's horrible! And Sandro forgave you for that? He really is sweet," I had to admit. "But that didn't actually *wreck* the car."

"Tsh, there's more," she said, dabbing the center of her lower lip, pouting at her reflection. "They got out of the box. I reached around to see what was goin' on, and look... millions of puppy scratches. Not to mention, the whole back, the floor, the seats, the doors, everything ripped to shreds, covered in pooh. Twenty minutes and the whole car was trashed. Have you ever *smelled* puppy pooh? *Inside* the stuffing of seats?"

Normally, this would be a near-tragedy. But I knew that within hours, Sandro would get "a deal" on a replacement.

"Shit, I hope this doesn't get infected," she said, rubbing in some glitter gloss just to be on the safe side.

We headed toward Elmwood Strip. Star Luxury was a two-story birthday cake iced in buttercream, on a manicured lot with a low iron fence. A golden awning was stuck over the door. Inside, warm Mediterranean colors lulled customers into loosening the grip on their wallets. The vestibule was silent, except for the piped-in sounds of surf and flute and dolphins critiquing each other's facials. I picked up a brochure and found the prices on the last page, as if the cost were unimportant. It was, in fact, astronomical.

"No problem," Vicky said loud enough for them to hear her in the back. "I've got Sandro's American Express. He says to make myself deleteriously happy with it."

"You mean deliriously happy," I said.

"Yeah, whatever."

The receptionist intimidated the hell out of me. She was a Ralph Lauren ad, only about twenty, but not too young to know she was fabulous. Tall and coltish, skinny black pantsuit, glossy sable hair combed into a severe ponytail, with the no-makeup look that takes lesser mortals hours to pull together. She looked us over and decided everything needed fixing. "Do you have an appointment? This will take some time."

"No, but we're thinking of having something waxed," I said, like I did it every day.

"What in particular?"

"Uh you know, Brazilian, of course, we do it all the time." *Are you crazy?* My chicken side shrieked. *You're going to pay a total stranger to rip all that hair off your privates? Knock me out with a frying pan first*!"

"We've just had a Couples Day cancellation, so we can fit you both in."

We trailed behind her past the treatment rooms, ducking in every open door to see if Honey was there. The pampered regular clients were in turbans and creamy terry robes, lolling on the thick cushions of white wicker chaises, cradling steaming cups of jasmine tea. Compared to them, we looked like somebody's social experiment lab project.

She led us to a brightly lit room, and told us to lie down in cotton gowns on side-by-side padded tables. Between us was a cart with an array of chrome tweezers and magnifying glasses, lined up like dental instruments. This was already seeming like a bad idea. I'm not a big fan of pain, especially my own. Especially when it involves the cold-blooded ripping out of the pubic hair whose first appearance is a moment of glory. But I did what she said, and let her hover over me with hot wax dripping off a tongue depressor.

"Lay off the underwear!" Vicky smacked away her aesthetician as she tried to pull off her panties.

"But ma'am, I can't wax it if I can't get to it. Or would you rather mail it in?"

"Oh hurry up, then. We shoulda done brows, Janice, I knew it," she frowned. "Brows, I can handle."

"A friend of ours comes here a lot," I began, making conversation with the girl who was going to make my Australian outback look like a plucked chicken. "Name's Sheila. It'd be great if she were here now...*yyyyowch*! What's wrong, did you have a fight with your boyfriend last night?"

"We don't discuss clients," the snippy little bitch said. I felt her spread more hot wax in my crotch and she ripped off another one, taking a big patch of skin with it. The searing pain made my teeth chatter.

"Easy on the whip! I'm not asking for her blood type." Well, *that* wasn't going to work. I looked over at Vicky, who'd rolled up a corner of sheet and was biting down hard on it. "Hey," I bluffed, "when we all had lunch together, didn't Sheila tell us she'd be here today?"

Vicky blinked. She'd gone deathly pale, and all the black liner had migrated in silent tears. She looked like Marilyn Manson. "That's it, I'm done!" she announced, spitting out the sheet and lunging for her jeans.

"But you're not!" the girl breathed, "you're lopsided, and I haven't even pulled this one off. There's still the other half!"

"No, there isn't. It'll stay hairy. Here," she said, tossing me my pants, "I just remembered something I forgot to do."

"What?"

"Anything."

"But then, how could we finish it?"

"Drunk."

We headed for the front, with the two white coats chattering behind us. Vicky used Sandro's card to buy us gift certificates for facials, and was just signing his name, when who should come around the corner looking all fresh-faced and innocent, but Honey Summer.

"Thank you very much, Ms. Fuoco," the receptionist crooned. "See you next week."

What to call her, Honey or Sheila? I went with, "Hi there, what a surprise!" She hiked up her Fendi and shoved the door open. Her image was completely different in a classy little designer outfit, a nice coral cotton Capri set with expensive silver flats. Her tan arms glistened with expensive body lotion. She looked confident and successful... and this time, alert. I wondered how much of our previous conversations she'd want to remember.

I told her I'd guessed she was the source in Johnny Renza's reports, but only guessed, because, "You're a very special woman, with unique attributes," whatever the hell that means. She was flattered. I said, "Renza is real worried that you might be in danger, because you probably have your own records of all the transactions. Do you?"

She answered straight out that she didn't, and frankly I couldn't imagine why she'd lie. She'd been so open about everything else, she'd want to take credit for that.

"Um, yeah," she said, "so now my problem is, with no records how can I locate all our customers, I mean, before somebody else does? How can they find *me*? I wish I'd done the interview with my face showing.

Now, My Apartment's going to get all the business. The girls can't date customers, but these aren't technically dates.... get it? And these girls recruit other girls, like the ones in Johnny's reports." Honey winked. "Now clients can't find me." Vicky and I traded looks. Could she be that stupid? Forget the publicity, the law would all over her. And for the cash flow potential of a prostitution operation that big, so would the mob.

Chills again. If the law was the least of *her* problems, it also was the least of mine. I was the one person who had access to absolutely everything of Siggy's, and everybody knew it. I told Honey now would be a good time to take a vacation.

"No way, not me, I can take care of myself!" She whipped out a nifty pearl handled .22 Beretta, and waved it at the car hop who was easing out of a sporty red 2007 Jaguar. "Ow!" A long fuscia nail got caught in the trigger, and she squeezed one off at the convertible top. The valet slammed the pedal down, and was still burning rubber with the door open when he ran the light on Miramar.

It was pure reflex that made me yank out my gun and point it at her. I didn't think she'd really meant to shoot the car, I'd had that nail problem, myself. We were five feet apart, locked in a standoff, holding each other hostage. A breeze kicked up, and it caught Vicky's double hoop wind chimes. She started chewing minus the gum. I could hear women coming out and knocking each other down to get back inside. Honey didn't look uncomfortable, and that worried me. I didn't like the way she wasn't even blinking.

"Okay, just slowly put it back in your bag," I told her, "and I'll put mine back too. No point doing anything else, right? On three. One, two," Honey shifted weight, "three." She didn't go for it. Trying not to wet my pants, I pretended it was a game.

"Okay now, sloooowly, here we go again," I said. When I got to three, we both inched our guns toward home. I had mine seated in the holster, but I wasn't turning it loose until her empty hand came back out of the Fendi. It came out, with a flash of metal. My fingers twitched on the

Sig... but it was only her car keys. Honey squinted at me and smirked. Her eyes didn't have that soft look anymore.

She said evenly, "You can tell Harold and his friends, they're done like dinner." She wheeled around to go find her pink T-Bird .

It was all making sense. Harold was about to lose his prostitution business to the mob. So was Honey. Naturally, a crooked cop would be their worst enemy, a double threat. But who was the cop? Did even Harold know? And if I needed police protection in this screwed up mess, who were the good guys? Part of me wanted to run to Tango and tell him yes, you were right, you do this, all of it, it's too much for me. The other part knew I'd never admit it. This was going to take a ton of chocolate.

I drove Vicky back to Balducci's. She'd had the time of her life. She was on the cell the entire ride, begging Sandro for a pearl-handled *anything*. He promised to look around, and I made a mental note to watch for gun shop robberies in the next twenty-four hours. I went home to figure out what I was going to say to Daly. As my key slid into the deadbolt, the voice I least expected whispered in my ear, "We have so much in common... why are we waiting?"

TEN

I ABOUT JUMPED OUT of my skin! My mind had been on Honey's chilling stare in the parking lot, and how I'd thought, just for a second, she was really going to shoot me and how I desperately didn't want to die. He put his hand on my shoulder and spun me around to face him. He kissed me hard, like his whole life was in it.

"Marry me," he breathed. I'd never seen him like this.

"How'd you get up here? You need an ElectroPass for the elevator."

"That's not the answer I was looking for. And call me Leon."

"Uh, Leon, what brought this on?" I asked as I opened my door. "We're friends, remember?"

"I realized when we were down at Smokes Creek with the bodies, after you interviewed me, that it was the longest you and I had talked in years. You stood on my foot so I couldn't leave. I know what that meant, and I liked it. You can do that any time. Don't stop after we get married."

"That was purely professional. We were talking about water-logged remains and sliced off body parts. That's not much to build a relationship on, do you think?"

"I know, but don't you see, we really have a lot in common. Like right now, we're both looking for Harold Sigmund, we're both investigators, we've known each other forever. I've always sorta been around, and your family really likes me. My mom and your Nonna get along great. They're both from Sicily. Your grandmother's taking her back to her roots." I did not consider this a plus. Nonna had turned Mamie into a poster child for *Goodfellas* reruns. That'll fly only so far, even in Buffalo.

"And," he went on, "here's the best part, I just got a promotion, a real good raise. So let's do it, Janice, whaddaya say?" He hooked his thumbs in his belt and waited. I'd never noticed his hopeful puppy eyes before.

I swallowed hard. Panic had become my natural state. If Ma ever found this out, she'd do cartwheels and back flips. Payoff for all the years of piano lessons, braces, classes at Miss Joelle's Academy for Young Ladies and Coke parties with pimply-faced Honor Society boys. Sweet, unsuspecting Leon had no way of knowing he had just asked for the hand of a woman who was a willing sucker for forbidden powdered sugar and hot Italian slacks – and who would stay that way for the foreseeable future. But I couldn't bear to bring a tear to those soulful eyes, so I said I'd think about it. He rocked up on the balls of his feet and kissed my forehead. He *had* to rock... I had a good two inches on him, without heels.

I shoved him out the door and reached for the phone. "Concierge? Oh, Javier, how are you? I just called to ask if my intruders are disturbing your sleep."

By the time I had lunch and showed up at Iroquois, it was nearly two in the afternoon. I slid the car up to the curb and felt déjà vu course through my veins. This time there was no Sweet Boy. No press pass. On general principles, I still was not putting money in the damn meter. There was almost nobody on the street, and the sidewalk was deserted. This car was all but invisible, anyway.

As I stood at the door waiting for Daly to buzz me in, I had the strangest sensation of being watched, like at the TV station just before my shootout with myself. I took a look around and casually raised my heel a few inches, to feel the reassuring weight of the gun just below my calf. The thick summer air stuck in my lungs. When the buzzer finally sounded, I leapt inside. Daly shouted down, "There in five, or would you rather come up?"

"I'll wait." Truth was, I would have been perfectly happy to go up, and to stay there until somebody found Harold.

"I was finished anyway," Daly said as he closed the door to the stairs and double-locked it behind him. "I just like to give you the option and see you squirm."

"You think you make me squirm? I can do it all by myself."

"Now that, I would want to watch." I bet he would. One word was all it'd take. This was my second stand-off of the day. Only this time if I blinked, I'd still win, and win bigtime. So really, why not give in? Some days you're just tired of fighting it... and some days you really need it. I was a big girl, I could handle a man like Tango Daly, I could keep everything in perspective. My eyes told him *Double dare you*. He could do with that whatever he wanted.

He wanted. He began by lifting my chin. His lips parted, and my mouth had no choice, it opened in response. His eyes turned a darker shade of green, and I imagined all the things he'd want my lips to do. I licked them, and he smiled. A knowing smile, a secret between us. My hand ran down the side of his neck, and discovered again how smooth and muscular it was.

I swallowed when he inched his finger along my throat to where that fourth sweater button should have been fastened, and hooked onto my bra. He pulled hard, and I leaned way in. I had to... my heels were caught in the bloody carpet again. It angled my butt out like a Victoria's Secret ad. I sucked in my stomach, and thought a mirror wouldn't be a bad thing. Slow drums were beating, Barry White was tuning up. *I wanted him*, with every bit of the yearning I'd been holding inside. Then something happened that I will never live down, if I live to be a hundred.

I farted.

And then I fainted.

When I came to, on the floor, Barry White had packed up and left me sitting with my head hanging between my legs. Through my hair, I could make out Daly's polished loafers.

"You were only out for a minute," he said. "It happens to the best of us. Of course when it happened to me, it was in the jungle right after a firefight, and I'd lost a lot of blood." He poked a Kleenex through. "And no, I did not fart myself off my feet."

"Thank you, I feel so much better knowing that." I blew a big one. "I need to talk, in case I pass out again."

"Thanks for the warning. I'll open a window."

"Smartass. Listen to me. I saw Honey, and it's all coming together." I filled him in on Star Luxury and the gun, about how she said she had no records, and I believed her. How she said Harold and his friends were done like dinner.

"And I've got one for *you*," Daly said, settling down next to me. "I've been told, by a very reliable source, somebody's had a sudden stroke of fortune, been bumped up the mob food chain. From soldier to associate. Pumping a drug and prostitution operation, very lucrative. Could be Honey's old friends."

"Drugs and prostitution do go hand in hand," I said. "Maybe Siggy, Harold and Honey had a silent partner who doesn't see the percentage in being silent anymore. I'm going to see Pop. And maybe Sandro." I tried to get up.

Daly rested his hand gently on my thigh. "You know, Janice, you can pull out of this right now, just walk away. You were hired to find Gerald Sigmund. He's been found. You're out, if you want to be." This wasn't like most other times we'd touched. Maybe there was room for a deeper relationship after all, the kind that lasts a lifetime. The kind that scares the bejesus out of me. He said, "I'm still in, because I have a score to settle. There's no discussion."

"Then I'm in, too," I said. I loved him for this. There was no discussion.

Outside, my heart stopped. The Toad had been towed. But it was only five spaces away, with a note on the windshield: "Next time, it'll be gone. So will your gun :-)" Officer Wolenski and his perennial problem with my firearms permit. A guy that jealous of somebody else's gun just has to have a problem firing his own.

It isn't only mothers who have radar. I hadn't even called first, and there was Pop, waiting outside the house for me when I drove up.

"Hey, little girl." He was a man of few words, spending days at home with two women. He was known to fall asleep waiting for breaks in the conversation.

"We better talk out here, he said softly. "Your Ma's nuts today... your grandma's *always* nuts." We leaned against the car, the way citizens of Iron Island have talked on hot summer days for generations. Pop, in his thread-bare undershirt and khaki pants, licked at the ink on his hands and stuffed them in his pockets. "Got somethin' to tell you."

"And I've got something to ask you," I told him. "Daly says one of the shiny suit crowd got bumped up. Please tell me it isn't Sandro. Actually, chances are better it's a cop, so please tell me it isn't Kielbasa."

"Sandro, I don't know about," Pop said. "Why not Kielbasa?"

"Don't tell Ma, but Leon came over today and he, uh, proposed. He got a little carried away 'cause he got a promotion and a raise. He thinks we belong together. And no, we don't."

"Aw geez, your Ma will know by sundown. They got an information chain longer than your sister's stockings."

"I don't have a sister."

"It's an expression. These dames know everything. You wonder when they do it, but I got it figured out. They talk so fast, their lips don't appear to be movin'."

"So what did you want to tell me, Pop?"

"Okay. I keep an eye on more than you think. I got a line on My Apartment. Now maybe you know more about this than I do, or maybe not." Pop changed weight to the other foot, and crossed his arms. "Dat place where you were almost roadkill has been linked to two murder-dismemberments, and the unsolved disappearance of a pretty nice lookin' kid, a nineteen-year-old by the name of Morgan Gelman, a.k.a. Bunny Tail. A dancer... and I use the term loosely. A case we've been workin' for years. We just nailed it. Unfortunately the perpetrator, well, she's about to get carted off in a Coroner's wagon. Looks like suicide. One Sheila Fuoco. Anybody you know?"

"*Sheila Fuoco?!*"

"Uh oh, fasten your seatbelt, it's gonna be a bumpy conversation." Ma was sailing toward us in her apron, walking fast with the big fork. Behind her, Nonna Giovanna and Mamie Kielbasa were hanging back, lined up on the front steps like crows. If the Old Country look was contagious, my mother was next.

"Ma, you don't by any chance have anything black in your closet, do you?

"Only for the Executive Game. Today, I'm thinking white." She made a cross with the fork. "Wedding white... and little pastel booties, Mrs. Leon Kielbasa, my smart, sensible daughter!" Pop shot me an anguished look.

"Wait!" Leon's mom rolled off the porch. "She's my daughter too, now!"

Nonna Giovanna, the main act, sprang to life. "Your wedding is the true expression of your love, Pommie. It'll be huge this season! It's this thing of ours. Time to settle some old scores, invite the right people. Round up the usual suspects!"

"*Casablanca?*" I raised an eyebrow to Pop.

"Yeah, somethin' new. I think she got a credit card," he whispered. "It's been rainin' Amazon DVD's. You drivin'?" He swung the car door open.

"Yeah, get in!" We careened around the corner and out of sight, leaving the three women on the lawn to make wedding plans and call anybody in Lovejoy who hadn't heard the news. I absolutely, positively was not marrying Leon Kielbasa. I knew it, Pop knew it. The only people who didn't know it were Leon and everybody else.

Access to the street where Honey Summer lived until about an hour ago was cordoned off for a block in both directions. A little much for a lone suicide, but this was no ordinary single twenty three-year-old. While she had frequent visitors, she'd been careful to keep a low profile on the street. She was the kind of girl neighbors would say kept to herself and didn't cause any trouble. The police obviously didn't agree. Six blue-and-whites were lined up, plus a black SUV that couldn't be anything but undercover. My heart lept into my throat when I saw that Frank Longoria was making a guest appearance in his dark blue Crown Vic.

I found him in the kitchen, deep in thought. I took a chance with, "Where is it, Frank?" He whipped around like he'd seen a ghost. He looked pale, bloodless, and it occurred to me he could be a quart low and I ought to be holding up a cross. For the first time, he didn't bite back. Maybe he was contemplating whether to carve me up or eat me whole. I eased out and made for the front room. The inside of the house looked like the outside, sad and neglected. What a horrible place to die.

Honey's room was at the end of the hall. I went in to have a look, and stepped into the Twilight Zone. Luxurious, claret fringed velvet draperies broke up bright purple walls. The polished walnut four-poster had a mattress just high enough to keep a girl's life interesting; and there were mirrors in enough places to make a person dizzy just getting up to shuffle to the bathroom. The drapes had been pulled and the room was dark, except for the crystal chandelier that threw teardrop shadows on Honey, who was sitting up in bed.

She was wearing the little coral number from three hours earlier. Her head lolled to the left, with a tidy round hole in the right temple. In her hand rested her pearl handled Beretta. It looked like all the pressure of the past few days had finally gotten to her. It *looked* like it. But when I'd last seen her, she'd been aggressively serious about being able to take care of herself.... and about Harold and his associates being in a world of trouble, which sounded a lot like a threat. Not the words of a despondent women.

Beyond that, there was one other small problem with this picture. Honey's gun was in her right hand. Most people are right-handed, but Honey wasn't. When she'd pulled that Beretta on me in the parking lot, it had been with her left hand. She hadn't shot herself. Someone had killed her.

"See? More in common every day." Kielbasa whispered in my ear, hot breaths tickling my neck. He was wearing fancy new musk after-shave, and he wasn't in uniform. Wow, that was some big promotion. So big, he was smooching me up at the feet of a murdered woman.

"Back off, little boy," Pop warned as he vice-gripped Leon's arm and yanked me into the hallway, "or I'll rat to your mommy." He was marching me toward the front door, when Longoria sidled out of the kitchen. "That does it," Pop growled. "I'm outside before I put my fist through somethin'. Hurry up."

"Too bad," Longoria said to no one in particular, when Pop was out of earshot. His eyes wandered the ceiling theatrically. "Such a pretty girl. Like so many ambitious young women, she had everything to live for. Then she went and killed herself. No one will ever know the terror of her final moments. Or what fate might now befall her loved ones." He fixed me with an icy blast that went right through my brain and flash froze it. My heart was going to pound itself to death. "Isn't that right, Janice?"

Some cerebral circuit must close when you expect cardiac arrest and it doesn't happen. It lit this redhead's fuse like a blowtorch, and hellfire shot out of my mouth.

"Piss off, Frank! I've got an ace you never dreamed of, and right now it's in four safe deposit boxes, in envelopes with four important addresses. Anything happens to me or anybody in my family, *your* family ain't gonna be too happy with *you, capice*? Best thing you can do right now is mind your own fucking business. Your ass is grass, and I'm the lawnmower!"

I stomped out to where Pop had the car idling. I didn't have four safe deposit boxes, or four anything, but it sure felt good to say it.

"Get in, Pommie," Pop said through gritted teeth. "I guess you're gonna have to make the call. I don't like it, but we got no choice."

I couldn't look at him. "Sandro, right?"

"Right."

Pop put the pedal to the metal as I punched in my cousin's number, glancing up just in time to see Johnny Renza's red Camaro fly past us toward Honey's house.

It had been two days since Honey's summer was cut short by a cold-blooded killer. Officially it was an ordinary suicide, if there is such a thing, and it didn't even make the papers. Who was I to ask to see ballistics reports, or to point out she wasn't even right-handed, and what would it get me? The hot weather doldrums had settled in, and the whole case was in suspended animation, along with Sheila Fuoco's body at the morgue. I hadn't heard from anybody... not Longoria, not Kielbasa, not even Harold. Sandro said he'd call back when he had something.

Oddest of all, I hadn't heard from Renza, who was the only other person I knew who'd spent quality time with Honey. We needed a reporter-to-reporter talk. After I peed in his hydrangeas, I swore I'd never go back; but what's the point of a guy being your first love, if he can't pony up the face time when you need it? So there I was, on his front porch again, in my excellent ruffled lime blouse, listening to the echo of his brass lobster door knocker at two-thirty in the afternoon.

I'd about given up hope of finding him home, when the door creaked open and a three-hundred-dollar Ralph Lauren cashmere robe stared back at me, with Renza crumpled up inside. I knew it cost three hundred dollars, because I'd given it to him the Christmas before I came to my senses and married Lou.

"Gawd Johnny, you look like De Niro. Y'know, in *Cape Fear*, the last part." Then I thought about my slacks. "Where's Thumper?"

"Back with Uncle Vinnie."

"Fair enough." I went inside. The place was a wreck. "You don't live like this, what's up? Your eyes are all bloodshot. Your hair looks like it got caught in an Edward Scissorhands drive-by." Johnny's notorious testosterone overload had fertilized a shaggy beard that took over the entire bottom half of his face. I had the impression if I turned him upside down, he'd look exactly the same.

He bit his lip. "It was my fault, Janice. She wouldn't have killed herself if I hadn't humiliated her in the series. Somebody must've recognized her. I talked her into it. But hell, I couldn't do it without her."

This was a sensitive side I hadn't seen in awhile. It made me wonder if there wasn't more between them. "You two didn't, you know, I mean you weren't actually fact-checking her fuzzy little girls, were you?"

"Fuzzy whats? Whatever you're thinking, it's nothing like that." Renza rubbed his eyes. "Honey was sweet, and the series made her look dirty. Well, it's a dirty business. But you have to be in the depths of despair to take your own life."

"Okay, read my lips," I said as I shoved a mess of potato chips and newspapers off the couch. "It's not your fault. Honey, or whatever the hell her name was, didn't kill herself, she was murdered. But not because she was a sweet little thing turning tricks. She and her friends were running a humongous prostitution ring. They're also Pharmaceuticals R Us. At least one of the girls at My Apartment got in the way, and Honey terminated her in a very ugly way. She was no angel. She made a lot of enemies, and one of them took her out. That's it, that's all."

Renza was speechless, helpless, just the way I like him. In a burst of compassion, I held him they way lovers do, and stroked his hair. He held me the way teenagers do, and stroked my boobs. Some things never change. "You want to feel sorry for somebody, Johnny? Try this on: you had the hottest story of your career, and you didn't even know it."

He sniffed and scratched his beard. "Not much of a reporter, am I? However, I do have some information that I'd like confirmation on. From you."

"What?" I asked, and got up to use the john.

"What's this I hear about you and Leon Kielbasa buying condoms at Eccola's?"

This is where I walked into the wall. "*What?* What are you even *talking* about?"

"My mom heard from your mom that you and Supercop are getting married. I just didn't know that buying condoms was part of the ritual. Where are you two registered, the Sheik aisle?"

"I'm going to kill him!"

"Leon?" he asked.

"Everybody!" I said. "Trust me, it's not what you think."

"How come *you* can say that, but you don't like it when *I* say it?" Renza smiled for the first time.

Junior Soprano started howling "Core N'grato", and I jumped to answer my cell. Sandro spat it out fast, in his raspy Jersey whisper: "Two things, and I can only say this one time, so listen up. One: The cop is Frank Longoria. Do not under any circumstances mess with this. Do not go near him. Do not do it."

"Wow, even for him, that's immoral," I said, speaking in code in front of Renza.

"Yeah, positively immortal. Two: Harold Sigmund is lookin' for you, and it ain't to talk. Don't be the hero. Go home and stay there. As we speak, Longoria is about to eliminate the competition, by neutralating Harold at My Apartment. Harold will 'resist arrest', *capice*? But if Harold wins, he'll be lookin' you up right after. So go home, lock the door and call that Daly guy, hear me? *Now!*"

"You mean neutralizing?"

"*Just do it!*" In the background, I could hear Vicky yelling that something was getting soft, hopefully it was ice cream. Then the line went dead.

This was the break I was looking for! I would be the reporter who found Harold Sigmund dead or alive, either way was fine with me. I did feel a pang of guilt as I blew out of Renza's place without explaining. After all, he *had* given me the Leonard Halley recapture story. Fortunately, the guilt passed.

I got hold of Smitty and bribed him with his weight in Molson and sausage to hijack the live truck over to My Apartment, and hang two blocks away until he heard from me.

"And I chose now of all times to lose weight," he said.

Then I made a courtesy call to Daly, and repeated everything Sandro had said.

"Where are you now?" he asked me.

"I'm going home. I've definitely had enough.". Right, home with a slight detour.

"Good girl. Stay there, I'm coming over."

Driving down Clinton toward My Apartment, I ran through different versions of how it could go. It wasn't just the story – or even the money -anymore, it was the chess game for survival. I was never any good at chess, but being furious ought to count for something. With luck, they'd blow each other into the next galaxy, and I'd get to cover the clean-up.

I dropped the car at a vacant tire shop, and Smitty waited in the news van nearby. I jogged over to the strip club. This time I was going in hands-free, with the phone clipped under my shirt so I could call Smitty when the time was right. My canister of Mace was right next to it. Out of habit I felt for my ankle holster, bucking a wave of nausea as I remembered the back room, and all the reasons I'd sworn never to carry

Daisy that low again. The entrance was wide open. Damian was probably in the men's room torturing the rats.

A car slowed, then speeded as I slipped into the deserted darkness. The stage would be on the right, the filthy couches on the left. *I'd pay a thousand bucks for a pair of gloves.* The music was pounding out my dental fillings. Before I could pick a place to hide, the mirrored disco ball and blue strobes jerked into action. I dived behind the couch nearest the wall, the one with the blotchy stains. *Do not let me throw up, not now. I swear I'll take Ma to lunch every week like a good daughter, if you just let me live through this. Nonna too. Well, maybe not Nonna.* The drums reached a trembling crescendo. *Okay, Nonna too.*

At this point, I was pretty sure I'd made a mistake coming back. I was positive, when my eye caught human movement in the doorway. A man was silhouetted just long enough to show he was big and sure-footed. He wasn't clumsy, so it wasn't Damian. He vanished in a heartbeat. I unholstered the Sig, held my breath and waited.

As strobe flashes bounced off the foot-wide rotating disco ball, blinding slivers of light pierced everything they could find. My mind started playing tricks. Damian was there, prying every corner of the room with his demented fiery eyes, then he vanished. I saw Honey crawling on the stage, moving to the music, provocative and sensuous. Longoria lingered close by, examining her. I rubbed my eyes and looked again. Honey wasn't there. But Longoria was. And the face caught in the lights was distorted with disgust and rage. He roamed the room like an animal, an animal with the sort of police training I didn't have, doing a sweep back and forth toward my end. I was terrified he'd actually be able to smell me. Had I worn perfume? Had I showered?

Finally, satisfied that he was alone, he turned to grope through the shadows to the right, heading toward the dressing room. He'd just touched the curtain, when the deafening music cut to silence. The loss of rhythm took him by surprise. It threw him off-balance, and he veered into a jumble of metal chairs. They came down like a pyramid of silverware, and took a long time to settle. This brought Harold onstage to see what was wrong. But he couldn't see, because the light was on his face... and on the monster revolver he was cradling in his right hand.

The metallic double-click of the slide on Longoria's semi-automatic loading one into the chamber caught Harold's ear. He whipped his gun level and fired blind in Longoria's direction. The blast reverberated off the walls, as Frank took his time carefully aiming to retaliate.

That was a split second before Smitty rang my cell, to see how things were going. In rapid succession, somebody clamped a hand hard over my mouth and my gun, and my phone was yanked off my waistband and sent skidding toward the stage. Daly whispered in my ear, "Don't move."

Harold swung toward us, then back to Longoria, and shot twice. Both rounds ricocheted with a crack off the chairs. Longoria rapid-fired back – five in a row – carving a nice little pattern into the butt of Harold's expensive slacks as he dived into the shadows. Frank's duty weapon would carry a minimum of ten rounds, so he had plenty left and he knew how to use them. Now they were exactly across the stage from each other.

"You're not going to steal my business, Frank!" Harold yelled. "We had a deal. It's you and me! You killed Gerald, I killed Honey, just like we planned. *I did it for us!* We're rich!"

"No deal. My friends reserve the right to change the rules while the game is in progress."

"Well they shouldn't have. Killing Norbert wasn't part of it," Harold said.

"He served a purpose, or his finger did. It pinned the murder on Halley. My idea. Good, huh?"

"*Tell them* we had a deal. They'll listen to you. They need you in this town! You can have Gerald's and Honey's two-thirds, like we said!"

"Not good enough," Longoria intoned. "They want it all."

My phone was still ringing. Unfortunately it was now within reach of Harold, who picked it up. Instinctively, I raised my loose hand to stop him, and he saw the movement. Smitty must have said something like, "The camera's ready to roll when you are," because Harold bellowed, "You bitch! Tell him to roll on *this*!" as he charged Daly and me, shooting up the couch.

Daly let go of my mouth, clamped his other big paw on my gun hand, and picked him off with two fast shots.

By the time Harold dropped, Longoria couldn't have been more than thirty feet away. Daly pulled back to draw his own weapon. I panicked and aimed my Sig at Frank. I peeled off three rounds and the ceiling chain exploded, sending the disco ball crashing down. He went splat in a sea of mirrors, jerked a couple times and went limp.

Daly got up and leaned over Longoria to check for vital signs. "Some you win, some you lose," he said.

"He's dead?"

"Nope, he's alive."

Then he took a closer look at the smoldering two inches of chain dangling from the ceiling, and whistled. "Well, I'll be. Were you aiming for the chain?"

"That would be on a need to know basis."

Then the man who saved my life wrapped me in his solid, strong arms and whispered low. "Next time, baby, keep your eyes open."

Smitty had picked up everything through my cell phone. All the cops had to do was follow his skid marks to the front door. By the time they cut their sirens at My Apartment, Smitty already had our camera gear on the sidewalk. The cops wanted to kick us off while they scraped a certain a homicide detective off the floor, but Mrs. Kielbasa's little boy Leon worked it out all for me. Plus, Leon had the yellow crime scene tape strung up so far from the building, the other stations couldn't cross it and needed binoculars to see what was going on. I decided to worry later about what that little favor was going to cost me. Hopefully it wasn't an engagement present.

We launched the live report that was going to put my career on the map with a dramatic full-screen shot of police and paramedics rushing the entrance of the club. The viewers couldn't see me, but they heard my very own, authoritative voice. I was going to narrate an award winner.

"This is PJ Santini reporting live from the scene of a fatal shootout at My Apartment. A lot more goes on at My Apartment than just clothes coming off. It's a lot more than a strip club." I winced, trying to focus. "I mean, My Apartment is home to illegal activities you'd never imagine, so close to where you live and bring up your children. Cocaine and even prostitution are easy to come by, at My Apartment."

At that point, Smitty hissed at the producer back at the station, "Holey moley, font the name of this joint! Explain what's going on!"

Some pimply intern who'd been in the news business exactly five minutes sat in the control room and typed the words that ran immediately at the bottom of television screens all over Buffalo: "Drugs Found At P. J. Santini's Apartment".

Smitty jerked the shot back and I was on camera, framed in the doorway, trying to wrench my foot out of my mouth. In the next few minutes, I recapped how Harold Sigmund had been importing cocaine, and how Honey Summer, a.k.a. Sheila Fuoco, had been running a prostitution ring. Unfortunately, neither was available for comment, as they were both dead.

I tap danced around how organized crime "allegedly" was trying to step in. On the spur of the moment, there was no way I could go deeper than that. Which was probably a good thing, since Longoria was still around. One way or another, he'd get a medal out of this. True, he had pinned Siggy's disappearance on Leonard Halley in order to shift attention away from his own involvement, but I couldn't prove that. I doubted Sandro would be interested in testifying.

It would come out soon enough that Siggy was involved... come out, that is, if I were to retrieve all the emails and other evidence from Daly's document safe, and do the story for enough money to open a Tiffany account. But first, my good friend Lenny Soper would have to cough up the bonus he promised me for finding Harold.

On the other hand, publicizing the fact that respected investigative reporter Gerald Sigmund had been the Big Kahuna behind all this, and had run it out of news department offices, would not be very good public relations, would it. So maybe Soper *wouldn't* pay. I wondered exactly *how much* he wouldn't pay... but then, blackmail is such an ugly word.

Renza must have shaved as soon as I left his house. He cut a real cute figure jumping the police tape, loping across the pavement all smooth and combed and firm in my favorite jeans. "Yo, Deadeye... nice shooting. I'm really proud of you!"

I put my hands on my hips, looking as elegant as I could with the whole world believing I was turning cheap tricks and dealing dope out of my apartment. "So Johnny, you uh, you heard about the disco ball?"

"What disco ball? Precinct says you saved Daly's bacon when Harold rushed him!" He swung me over in a showy Hollywood kiss. I could hear my vertebrae clicking into place.

Daly took half a step toward us "Precinct says *what*?" He'd begun shallow breathing. His fingertips were brushing, available to go anywhere at a second's notice. I didn't think he even knew he was doing it.

I straightened my shirt. Renza helped. Then my out-of-control tongue ran a wet line around my lips. "Wow. It sure is hot."

"We could go for some celebratory beignets, when I've filed my story for the five o' clock," Renza said, making meaningful eye contact. "We have things to talk about, you and I. Meet me after, Janice?"

"Um, I'll see," I said glancing sideways at Daly. "There's some paperwork at the office." It was true. There's a mountain of explaining after a private investigator fires a weapon on the job. "Gunplay certainly is... exhilarating," I said, blowing hair off my sweaty face.

We climbed out of Daly's nice, cool BMW and made for the back door of Iroquois Investigations. I hung back a few paces, trying not to breathe the haze of tar-scented heat bouncing off the blacktop. Daly entered the code to disarm the security system. He changed it every week, and was the only person who knew it. There was not one square inch of his office that wasn't covered by a motion detector, camera and microphone. Every move, every sound could be digitally recorded. I often wondered whether he ever just happened to accidentally turn it on when we were together.

"Nervous?" he said sideways.

"'Course not. Been here a million times. But then, those other times the lights were on."

He walked ahead. "You're not a sissy. You think gunplay is exhilarating, remember?"

I'll tell you what was exhilarating. The smell of Daly in the dark, after our close call. And the feel of silk slipping across his bicep, when I caught myself as the carpet grabbed my shoe. "Aren't you ever going to change this darn rug?":

"Are you always going to have to go shoeless in people's offices? Adapt. Improvise." I could hear him smiling.

He wasn't getting reaction that easily. I was all business when the lights came on. "So the whole thing is wrapped up," I said. "Honey's dead, however she got that way. Gerald Sigmund and Norbert Dojka are outta here. Harold's definitely dead, let's not go into who thinks *what* about how that happened. Where's the paper I have to sign?"

Daly strode around his desk to pull out a set of keys and open a file cabinet. With everything that had gone on, I hadn't noticed his slacks. They were new, a real dark gabardine houndstooth that moved a little after he stopped, trying to decide where to settle on his fine body. He laid the case out.

"Bottom line: Harold hired you to get records of prostitution contacts, and the financial books, before the mob could appropriate them.

It *was* a race, he was using you. He wanted you with him when he identified the finger, so he'd go on record as being surprised and horrified. I'm impressed with the way you hung in, even though you could have gotten yourself killed. Ironically, most of the information was out in the open. I'm keeping everything in deep storage. Someday Longoria will trap himself, and I'll be there."

He looked back down at the folder with all the forms to fill out, and closed it. "We'll do this tomorrow."

On the way up, he examined the ruffles of my shirt, evaluating the difficulty level of the buttons. I went for the crystal paperweight, just on general principles. He locked his grip onto my wrist. It felt like a million bucks.

"Whew! Is the air conditioner working?" My bangs were glued to my forehead.

The gabardine shifted as he swung around the desk, and pressed against me. His heat nearly melted my half-mowed lawn. "One kiss, Janice, then you decide," he exhaled. This time, I was definitely not biting his ear. Somebody whimpered, I think it was me, as my lips settled on his. The kiss was really hard, but not as hard as his Howitzer.

Then he did the unfairest thing he's ever done. He held my head in his hands. Head holding is a male end-run around a woman's natural defenses. It makes a woman think of love instead of sex, and of course love *leads* to sex. "You know," he said, "upstairs is a restricted area. I was wondering if you'd like an official tour. If you get thirsty, there's Dom Perignon. If you get hungry, the Beluga's on ice, too."

"Tango..."

The real question now wasn't life or death, it was far more important: Beignet or Beluga?

THE END

Turn the page for a preview of

Heels of Fortune

the new second book of Lynne Russell's
PJ Santini series!

ONE of HEELS OF FORTUNE

"I WEEL SUCK ON YOUR poosy until your ears flaap like those of an elephant!" the deep voice intoned over bump-n-grind background music that bore a striking resemblance to Hockey Night In Canada. The call was coming from my parents' house.

"Nonna, is that you? Hello, Nonna Giovanna? Why are you calling, are you alright?"

"*Aspetta*, wait... no no, not you my love..." she said to the man at her end, then the line went dead. My transplanted Sicilian grandmother was discovering amateur dubbed-in American porn, and the family was trembling at the possibilities.

That's what you get for answering the phone in church, I told myself. But it was the other call that really started the trouble. It came so soon, I thought it was Nonna again.

"Not now. I'll call you back," I whispered.

“You have something that doesn’t belong to you. I want it.”

“Excuse me?” The last time somebody said that to me, it was that bitch Kathy Shula in the parking lot during Senior Prom, trying to repossess the captain of the hockey team. She'd been way overreacting. I was only borrowing him.

“I’ll put it in short headlines, so you can understand,” he said dryly. “Your husband thought there was only the Polaroid. But there’s a cod, a memory cod. You give me the goose, I’ll give you the cod.”

“Cod. Is this about fish?”

"The carrrd, the memory carrrd!"

"Oh, *carrrd.* Are you from Boston? Who is this? Is this that 1-900-SexTalk number I accidentally dialed last week? You know it's illegal to keep calling me back."

"Remember, you're in the picture, too. If you don't give me the goose, the cod will go to your friends at the Precinct, and I promise you, it will take... you... down. You'll never know what hit you. You have 48 hours. I'll be in touch."

"Wait! What am I, a farmer? I don't have any goose. You have the wrong number."

"No I don't, Ms. Santini, I'm looking right at you."

"Who are you?" I demanded whipping around, frantically craning my neck to search faces. But nobody had a cell phone to his ear. He'd already hung up. About that time, the church minister walked to center front, stretched out his arms, bent his knees and made palms-down movements, his eyes fixed on some distant, imaginary chopper he was guiding in for a landing. This being a room full of TV people, it takes more than that to shut us up. So he began flapping in slow motion like an Animal Kingdom lake bird. The effect was curious enough that people did start paying attention. And snickering.

We had gathered there to bury our own twisted television colleague, Gerald Sigmund, "Siggy", who'd been running a monster drug and prostitution ring off of his humble newsroom computer. It had gotten him dead. I'd become involved in that case both as a reporter and as a private investigator, but all that was finished now. The only things that were left were spent bullet casings from one end of Buffalo to the other, and glass shards that I was still pulling out of my head from a terrifying episode in a strip joint dressing room.

Droplets of perspiration were running through the expensive *M*A*C* foundation on my upper lip, which did not improve my mood. The stranger on the phone had made me feel really pissy. It's not good to feel pissy at a funeral. So I leaned to my right and decided to take it out on another of his gender.

"Pssst, hey. It's sweltering in here! Was it absolutely necessary for me to wear all this bedroomy crap?" I complained into the man's smooth, tan cheek. I watched the back of his hand slide up and down my arm, and it gave me the shivers, the sort of shivers that make your pupils dilate and drool slide out the corners of your mouth.

"All I suggested was the color," he said without looking. "Two layers of lace and long sleeves was *your* idea. So take one of them off."

"Smartass. You know the bottom one is underwear. This was all I had in black. Except for my Catwoman outfit, which would've set the pews on fire."

I didn't think people had to wear black to funerals anymore, but when have I ever said no to Tango Daly, the architect and owner of Iroquois Investigations, and the hottest private detective boss on the planet? Alright, I have, but it's torture every time. So I've developed a hard and fast rule about hard, fast ones like Daly: When I start fantasizing about a possible future, any possible future, I picture myself a year down the road, seven months pregnant, standing in a pink terrycloth robe and fuzzy scuffs in a laundry room, spot-cleaning his Jockeys. I'm allergic to that. But then my little internal voice starts up. *You know if it were Daly, you'd like it. He'd have you propped up on the dryer, diddling your spin cycle, and then...* then I tell the bitch to shut up.

The hot ground by the casket sucked up my black patent leather stilettos like soft cement. Sweat trailed down the center of my back, as I made an unsteady effort to shift my weight without leaning on either Daly or Renza. Both would consider that foreplay.

An hour later, we'd wrapped it up and everybody was grateful to be headed out, when a guy shouted over from three tombstones away.

"Hey! Do I look crazy to you?" I wouldn't say his eyes were spinning around like Marty Feldman's, but it was hard to tell which one was looking at me.

"That would depend on your definition of crazy," I told him.

"They're trying to make me believe I'm insane, but I'm as solid as you are."

As me? That would be a problem. "How can you tell?" I shouted back. "Everybody who's crazy swears they're not."

He dragged his shovel over and leaned an elbow on it, while he wiped sweat out of his eyes with the back of his other hand.

"Well, I know what I know. I dug my ass off last night getting a plot ready for today, and today the damn thing isn't here. It's gone."

Made in the USA
Columbia, SC
26 May 2019